Just Sisters

By Carol Paxman

You can connect with Carol on her website at www.carolpaxman.com, or find her on Facebook or Twitter.

To receive advance notification of new releases and free books, sign up for my newsletter here.

Cover by rebecacovers

For my sisters, the ones born to me and the ones I chose. My life would be so empty without you.

And for Hailey, always for Hailey.

Momma's J Girls

Where is Daddy? He has to be here, everyone is talking about him. Why are they crying? I'm starting to get scared.

I ask Momma where my Daddy is, she hugs me and smiles. It's that funny smile, the one I don't understand. Momma is crying too. Grammy picks me up and pushes my hair out of my face.

“Poor little thing, it's gonna be ok.” She says. What's going to be okay? Pop Pop takes me outside to play. I don’t want to play, I want my Daddy. I run back in the house, looking for him. My Daddy will make everyone stop crying, my Daddy always makes everyone laugh. He can even make Momma laugh when she is mad at him.

More people are coming in, some of them I know, most of them I don't. Everyone is hugging me, too tight, too many people. I wish they would stop. I'm scared. I hear Grammy tell Momma to settle down, think about the baby. Now I'm really scared, is Neenie gone with Daddy too?

I want Daddy, I want Neenie, I want these people to go home and stop making Momma cry.

My sister's name is Jeanie but I couldn't say it for a long time so I called her Neenie, now everyone else does too. Momma says Jeanie and I are Irish twins, whatever that means. All I know is Jeanie is my best friend. I ask Momma where Neenie is, she tells me Neenie is sleeping, and not to wake her.

Momma always says that because Neenie is a cry baby. Pop Pop says it's because she is too little to know happiness and that I need to teach her. I know Neenie cries because Momma and Daddy yell a lot. Neenie gets scared when they yell. I don't, cause I'm bigger.

I run down the hall to find my sister. I know she will be scared if she wakes up and the house is full of strangers, then she will start crying. I hate when Neenie cries. It always makes me sadder. I climb in Neenie's crib. Momma will be mad. She says Neenie and I are both too big for cribs. We will be three and four soon, but Neenie loves her crib and I love Neenie so I climb in anyway.

Neenie is sleeping, sprawled out on her back, her raggedy lambie next to her head. I want to wake her up and make sure she is okay, but I know Momma will be mad. I listen to the grown-ups, I can't really hear what they are saying, just the noise of so many people in the house. My thumb finds its way to my mouth, something else Momma doesn't like, and I fall asleep twirling Neenie's hair.

For the next several days our house was always full of people, everyone but my Daddy. Grammy said he went to live with the angels.

There was a funeral. Neenie and I were all dressed up and everyone kept calling us poor little angels, which confused me even more. If Daddy was living with the angels and Neenie and I were angels, why wasn't Daddy there?

Our Momma got fatter and fatter, she explained that her last gift from Daddy was growing in her belly, a baby brother or sister for us. When Momma went to the hospital to have Janie I was scared she was going to have to go live with the angels too. Instead we got a new sister.

Momma brought Janie home from the hospital by herself. Grammy and Pop Pop didn't drive so when it was time for the baby, Momma drove herself to the hospital then drove herself home afterward.

I didn't really understand at the time that my Daddy wasn't ever coming back. Momma said he got hurt at work and had to go be with the angels and that he would always watch over us.

Neenie and I were excited when Grammy told us we had another sister. Of course, at three and four we were expecting a playmate. Not a screaming, red faced, smelly lump. When Momma showed us Janie for the first time, Neenie and I both said "Take her back." Momma explained that we were her J girls, we had to stick together and watch over each other and make Daddy proud. None of that made sense, we just wanted that baby to stop crying.

After Momma brought Janie home from the hospital she cried a lot and Janie cried a lot. It seemed like someone was always crying and I blamed it all on Janie. She made my Daddy go away and now she made my Momma cry. I didn’t like this new life without Daddy, and I didn't like the new sister I got in his place.

As Momma became more and more lost in herself and Grammy took over the majority of Janie's care, Neenie and I were left to our own devices.

Momma said not to play by the creek, but we did anyway. We were very careful, until Neenie fell in. I had to fall in after her because I didn't know how else to get her out. The water kept going up my nose and in my eyes, and I couldn't keep my head above the water. I could hear Neenie crying when my head came up, but I couldn't see her. I tried to call for her but that just made the water go in my mouth. After being tossed by the water, when I'd forgotten which way was up and which way was down, I felt someone grab my hair.

Neenie saved me that day. My baby sister managed to get herself wedged in some branches and she grabbed my hair and pulled me to her. We stayed out for a long time that day, until our clothes were dry so no one would know we fell in the water. If they knew they would make us stay inside and tell us to be good girls and not worry our mother so much.

We didn't think Momma worried about us so much anymore. We didn't really think Momma thought about anything. Most of the time she just stared out the window, like she was waiting for Daddy to come home. It gave me hope. If Momma was waiting for him then I decided Daddy was going to get away from the angels and come back to us, we just had to be patient.

Momma had moved us both into twin beds when she got fatter with Janie, said the crib was for the baby not us because we were big girls. We pushed those beds together after Neenie saved my life. We needed to be able to hold hands so we could sleep. Neenie said she dreamed she missed my hair and I just kept floating down the river and she screamed and screamed but Momma never came. I dreamed that Neenie would leave me and I would be alone with Momma and Janie. I wanted to hold onto her so I could make sure she didn't leave while I was sleeping.

Preparing for the worst

Infertility is like a death sentence. Maybe the governor will come through for you, and maybe he won't. I know that sounds dramatic, but five years of struggling to conceive has colored my world view. I feel like my life is on hold. We can't plan a vacation too far in advance because what if I'm pregnant and can't fly? A glass of wine? At this point in my cycle, I don't think it's a good idea. Going to the gym might help burn off some of this nervous energy, but what if I'm pregnant and I do something that will jeopardize the baby? Every tiny decision is run through the lens of where I am in my cycle and the possibility of pregnancy. Most days it just makes me even crazier than all those hormones that are injected into my body every month.

One of the hardest parts of this whole thing is that other people keep having babies. I get invited to baby showers and birthday parties. I don't want to go but all of my excuses sound lame. How can I make people understand that seeing their perfect, beautiful babies makes me so, so angry? What kind of human being is angry about children? An infertile one. A bitter, bitchy infertile human being. That's me.

It's hard to always be happy for someone else when I can never be happy for myself. I don't understand it, and I'm furious at my body for betraying me. Teenage children conceive, carry, and give birth to babies every damn day. But I can't. People abuse, mistreat and otherwise destroy the one thing that I spend every waking moment wishing for. How is this fair?

This is the reason I'm in Todd's truck, loaded down with boxes, and headed to visit my sisters. It's time to try to make up for the bitch I'm about to become.

I wish it wasn't like this. I love my nieces and nephews, but every time we have a failed pregnancy attempt I can't stand the sight of them. I feel like the worst person in the world that I can't be happy for my sisters and their children when my heart is shattered. I've tried so hard to act like everything is normal when that test comes back negative, but

I can't and I don't want to take my bitterness out on the kids. So I spoil them a little to make up for the next two weeks when I won't see them. After tomorrow, the sight of these happy, smiling babies that I love so much will reduce me to tears.

Over the weekend I went to my favorite make believe store, Wish Upon a Star. I got knights, damsels in distress, and for my littlest nephew, froggy pajamas. I pulled up in front of Julie's house. Her twins, Sam and Max are watching for my car. I called them last night and told them I had a surprise. They love surprises, and I love these little monkeys. They run out the door like the house is on fire.

"Aunt Jeanie, Aunt Jeanie, where's our surprise?" Both boys are jumping and tugging on me, trying to be the first to see their surprise.

"My, my, little boys without manners. Hmmmm, maybe I should take all the surprises to Aunt Janie's kids, I bet they have some manners." I loved teasing the boys. Julie's kids were the best behaved five year olds I'd ever seen. The boys stopped jumping long enough to give me a hug and kiss and let me get the box out of the truck. I loved elaborately wrapping their presents and then having them try to guess; that was half the fun of buying them something. Janie's kids were still too young to be very inventive at guessing, but they were catching on.

Julie was watching us from the front door. My sister was, as always, remarkably put together for someone who worked at home while entertaining twin boys. I don't think I have ever seen my sister's house a mess, even after having the boys. She came home from the hospital and it was business as usual. Janie and I joked that Julie read the boys their schedule every day before they were born so they would know what was expected of them. Julie is organized, efficient, and wastes no time taking care of business. No lollygagging about for my sister.

“What have you done this time sister?” Julie hugged me, then stood back to look at me. I knew she was looking for anything that was different, anything that would tell her that maybe, just maybe, this time would work for me. Oh how I wish there was something to see.

“Spaceship, is it a spaceship Aunt Jeanie?” Sam asked.

"No, it's a race car!" Fast cars, that was our Max.

"I know, it's a swimming pool." Sam guessed. "Or maybe a kitty cat, I've wanted a kitty my whole life." Sammy's serious little sad face made me laugh, I picked him up and hugged him.

"Your whole life, bud? That's a way long time, I don't know how you've survived." I kissed his chubby little cheek.

"Not a kitty, kitties are dumb. Maybe a big dog that we can ride, like Clifford." Now Max was excited, he had just discovered Clifford and he was almost as cool as fast cars.

"Okay, doesn't look like you can guess this time either so once again, I am the coolest aunt ever, so don't forget it. Open your present, I'm so excited for you to see what it is."

The boys tore into the box, throwing tissue paper everywhere, pulling out suits of armor, head gear and the like. I had hidden the stick horses in the bottom of the box under a false bottom, so I knew it would take them a minute to figure it out.

“What time do you go in tomorrow?” Julie asked, picking up the tissue paper.

“6 am for blood work, results by noon. I'm not getting my hopes up, this time doesn't feel any different than the other two. Todd wants to consider our other options.”

“I thought you guys weren't ready to adopt? I think it's a great idea but last week when we were at your house for the barbeque you didn't seem ready.”

“I don't think I am, and I don't think Todd is either. We talked with the doctors last week, we still have six frozen embryos. So far, our embryos have been healthy and viable, it's just me. All the tests, procedures, and money we've spent and I haven't gotten pregnant once. They don't know why, but the doctors suggested we might have better luck with a surrogate.” I was nervous, neither of my sisters had been very receptive about a surrogate before. I was hoping I could change their minds.

"Isn't that risky? I know it doesn't happen a lot, but I'm always heartbroken when I hear about a couple that used a surrogate and at the last minute she changed her mind. That would be horrible and really Jeanie, after everything you've been through I don't know how you would survive something like that."

I knew Julie was trying to look out for me. That's her job, she takes care of everyone, but I have to do this, for me. "Everything we've done is risky, all the procedures carry their own risks, including in vitro. Every time I take hormones to stimulate my ovaries it increases my risk of ovarian cancer. Nothing comes easy, but one thing in our favor is that we have twelve frozen embryos. If a surrogate gets pregnant with one of our embryos then the baby will be our biological child so that lessens the legal complications."

"But?" Julie knows me too well, "I hear a 'but' in your voice."

"Well, I'm trying to come to terms with the fact that I may never experience a pregnancy, that's hard to wrap my brain around. Women's bodies are built to grow our children and I may never get to know what that feels like. It's almost like a death, but in a different way. I realize that I have to let that dream die if it's standing in the way of having a child. The child is what's important, not how it gets here. I don't know if I'm ready to give that up though. I've loved getting to experience pregnancy through you and Janie, but I want my own experience."

"I guess I can understand that, although I could have gone my whole life without stretch marks and a bladder that has forgotten its purpose in life." Julie laughed, she always tried to make light of things but we both knew it was a fine line. What was bothersome about pregnancy to her was something I couldn't help but be jealous of, so we didn't talk about it much. Early on my sister's would complain about their pregnancies, the stretch marks, morning sickness, and labor. After about two years of trying to have a baby my sisters stopped complaining. At least when I could hear them, anyway.

I never wanted to be that stereotypical infertile woman that everyone tip toed around but, like it or not, I'd turned into her and I wasn't sure what to do about it.

“No freaking way!” That was Max, and from the fire shooting from my sister's eyes, I knew he was in big trouble.

“Maxwell Benjamin, right here, right now!” Julie ran a tight ship and Max came barreling around the corner, even though he knew he was in big trouble. “Young man, what did you just say?”

“I'm sorry Mommy.” Max’s eyes were filling up and I saw they had discovered the stick horses. They were probably what caused Max's reaction.

“I didn't ask you if you were sorry, I asked you what you said. Repeat it please.”

“I can't remember.” Max's little lip was quivering, but he saw the look in Julie's eye. “I said freaking Mommy, I'm sorry.”

“Why are you sorry? Do you remember why we don't say those words?”

“They don't mean anything good, swear words are used instead of real words and they are hurtful.” Max was holding tightly to his stick horse, afraid his punishment would be the loss of this wonderful plaything.

“Let me see, buddy,” Julie said to Max. Although she was strict, my sister wasn't an ogre, “That is way cool! I can see why you got carried away. Give me a hug and go chase your brother on your horse. I know you will be more careful choosing your words next time.”

Max's little face lit up and he threw himself at Julie, “Thanks Mommy, I promise, no more swears. Sam, did you get your horse out?” And Max was off and running.

“I love the costumes, where do you find those things? I've never seen stick horses that actually have a body.”

“Wait till you see the girls, they are damsels in distress and I found Rapunzel wigs. I know I'm mixing things up, but can you see Lacey and Brie dragging four foot long wigs behind them? I giggle every time I think about it.”

Julie laughed, “Knowing Janie, she will have a castle constructed out of cardboard boxes so the girls can let down their hair.”

“I better get going, still need to stop at Janie's and give her kids their toys. Don't call tomorrow. You can come over if you want, but don't call. I won't answer.” I walked to the front door and called the boys for a final hug and kiss.

Julie's look told me she thought I was being too negative, “Sister, you have to think positively, this time could be it.”

“And it also might not. I know you think I'm being negative, I'm sorry, I'm not like you, I can't just keep smiling until something good happens. I tried, it just made it harder when things didn't work out. I have to be realistic. All I can do is try everything that is available to me and keep moving forward."

I picked up each of my nephews who hugged me tightly and thanked me for the horses and swords. As soon as I put them down they were off, back to their game of make believe.

"Hope for the best, but plan for the worst." Julie smiled sadly, "I can't wait until you can just plan for the best. I love you sister, be safe." Julie hugged me, trying not to let me see the tears.

I blew her a kiss and quickly turned and walked across the porch and down the sidewalk to the car. I watched Julie close the front door and saw her shadow move into the family room with the boys.

Please sister, I thought, *decide you want to be my surrogate so I don't have to ask*. I started the car and headed to Janie's.

Please don't judge me

I knew before I heard her at the front door that Jeanie had arrived. My kids adore her, so the squealing and jumping up and down at the window started as soon as they saw Todd's truck. My sister was wrestling several different sized boxes out of the back of the truck. I pasted on my best happy-to-see-you face and opened the door. "Wait here guys, Mommy's going to help Aunt Jeanie," I said to the kids and went out the front door and down the walk, laughing as my sister tried to juggle everything.

"Hey Sister, sometimes you just need to ask for help. What in the world is it this time? Should I be afraid?"

"Jules didn't call and tell you? Good, I want you to be surprised too. Oh, Porter's outfit is on the front seat, can you grab it?"

We managed to half drag, half carry the loot Jeanie brought for the kids up the walk and into the house. I knew she was doing this in case things didn’t go well tomorrow, it would be hard for her to see the kids for a while. It always was. I wanted to talk about it, I wanted Jeanie to know that I was praying that this time would be the time she had waited for. I never knew what to say or how to say it, so I avoided talking about it.

Plus, I couldn't help but feel a little bit guilty, all Bryan had to do was look at me and think about sex and the next baby was on the way. It wasn't fair, and I hated being a reminder of what Jeanie didn't have.

The kids climbed all over Jeanie, I tried to pry my littles off her legs. “Hey guys, settle down or Aunt Jeanie won't be able to give you your presents. Don't you want to see what you got?”

“Who’s gonna guess this time? What do you think I brought you?” Jeanie sat on the floor with Brie, the two year old, in her lap.

“Pwesents?” this from Brie, who wasn't quite sure how the game was played.

"Yes, baby, I brought you presents, but what's in those presents?"

"A new wheel for my bike?" Collin, my four year old, had left his bike in the yard and someone rode it and broke one of the training wheels off, I hadn't had a chance to get a new one yet.

"That's an awfully big box for a wheel Collin," Jeanie said, "What else could be in there?"

I went into the kitchen to pour some tea for us while the kids took turns guessing. When I walked back into the room with our drinks, Jeanie decided the kids had guessed enough and started handing out boxes.

"Where's Munchkin? I bought him the cutest froggy pajamas."

"Finally napping. I think he's getting molars or something, all he does is chew and cry. Lately he's been chewing on Brie because she is the only one he can catch. Makes for a long afternoon!" I laughed. My kids are a crazy, noisy bunch but I love them.

"Wait, isn't this a sippy cup minus the lid?" Jeanie looked a little confused.

"Sorry we built a fort out of boxes in the basement and I didn't run the dishwasher, but in this house, we always have enough sippy cups."

Jeanie gave me that look, the one that said, 'isn't it time for you to grow up and mother these kids?'

Before she could start the lecture, I jumped right in to help Brie open her box, exclaiming all the while.

"Holy cow! This is the coolest thing ever! Thanks Aunt Jeanie, it's even better than a new wheel!" Collin was so excited about his stick horse that he took off running and proceeded to knock Brie over with the back end of his horse. Brie's howls woke Porter.

"It's ok sweetie, brother was just excited, it was an accident. Come love your sister, Collin." I was trying to calm Brie down, and I could hear Porter calling for me. He hadn't yet started crying but would soon if I didn't get up there.

"Collin, come apologize to your sister, you knocked her over and made her cry. If you can't play nice we will have to take your horse away." Jeanie was calling Collin over. I hated when my one of my sisters disciplined my children. Their rules were not my rules. In our house, we focused on love.

Trying to head things off, I picked up Brie. "Let's go get your brother so he can see what Aunt Jeanie brought for him too, he will be so excited." I headed out of the room as if I hadn't heard Jeanie, and Collin hadn't heard her over his own horse noises and Lacey's excited squeals.

I picked the baby up, well, the baby so far. I still wanted at least two more, even though my sisters thought I was crazy. We didn't talk about it much anymore and it hurt that I had to hide my joy in my children. Every time I got pregnant, I could see the hurt and disappointment in Jeanie's eyes. I tried to downplay my pregnancies, saying things like "You would think I would have figured out what causes this by now."

I felt like a traitor to my babies but I was trying so hard not to hurt my sister more than necessary. I can understand Jeanie being upset, but I hate that I have to downplay my joy. Jeanie's sadness is hard but Julie just makes me feel like I'm failing as a Mom, all the time. Just because my way isn't her way didn't mean my way is wrong, but I can't seem to convince her of that.

"There is my little Munchkin, come to Aunt Jeanie." Jeanie held out her arms for Porter.

"He's soaked through, let me change him first." I plunked Porter on the floor in the family room and started pulling his wet clothes off. I reached over to grab a pair of pants out of the laundry basket on the floor and laughed at my older kids joy at their gifts. Brie and Lacey are tripping over each other's wigs. "Where did you get those wigs? They are hysterical!"

"Do you think that's a good idea?" Jeanie was looking down at me with a concerned look on her face. "I'm sure it's not sanitary for the other kids."

I realized she was talking about changing Porter on the floor in the family room, just one more thing that I didn't do right. I tossed the diaper in the trash can in the corner. We have two kids in diapers full time and one prone to accidents so there is a trash can for wet diapers in each room. Bryan empties them every night. "Really? Are you worried about the kids, the carpet or you? This is my fourth, Jeanie, I've managed to keep them all alive. God only knows how, but I've done it. These kids have peed on each other, pooped in the tub when they are all in there, vomited on each other, and eaten from the same spoon. I don't think it will kill them if I change their brother's wet diaper in the middle of the floor." I finished changing Porter and got up to go wash my hands. Why did she have to suck the joy out of me?

“Janie, you know I didn't mean it like that. I just think that things would be easier for you if you were a little more organized, had the kids on some kind of routine.” As Jeanie was saying this the kids were jumping from one piece of furniture to the next because the dragon- Porter- lived in the moat, the moat was the floor, so you couldn't touch it. There was lots of screaming, especially when one of the girls tripped on their wig and fell in to the moat. I absolutely love my children's imaginations and encourage them every chance I get.

“Easier for who? Do I look like I'm having a hard time? I know you and Julie don't believe it but I love this. I love the noise and the mess and the constant motion; I love it all. When my kids go to bed at night, or they are all down for a nap at the same time, I'm lost. I need their chaos, it makes me a better mom. They encourage me, they inspire me to think outside of the box. We have fun, we laugh, no one gets yelled at or punished; isn't that what childhood should be instead of what we had?”

I could see that I had hurt Jeanie by reminding her of what she didn't have. Sometimes I got so tired of tiptoeing around everyone's feelings when they certainly never considered mine. Both of my sisters believe that I am unorganized, lazy even, and it was just a matter of time until something terrible happened to one of my children. “I'm sorry sister, I'm just a little cranky. I haven't been feeling completely up to par today. I know you are just looking out for me, but really, I'm fine, the kids are fine and when it is all beyond my control you will be the first person I call, okay? Now let's go slay some dragons!” I picked Porter up out of the moat and started flying him around the room, pretending to get the bigger kids.

Jeanie relented and started helping the princesses escape the crazy dragon while Collin did his best to slay us all with his foam sword. After about fifteen minutes, my sister flopped on the couch.

“I really have no idea how you keep up with all of them Janie, I'm exhausted!” At least Jeanie was smiling again. “I gotta go, I didn't realize how late it's getting. I love you, sister. Come kiss me kids, I gotta run.” The kids all came running up to hug Jeanie and thank her for the toys. “Stop and see me this week, you know I won't be up to calling but I'd love to see you. Just you. Love you sister." And with that, my sister was out the door and on her way to her perfect, color-coded world.

I must have been the milkman's child because I have nothing in common with these sisters of mine. Who cares if your spices are alphabetized when you could be reading Little Red Riding Hood and using your best voices?

Turning back to my children, I picked up Porter and we started playing again,

Tiffie LaBell

"Janie, look, I gotta run, the boys are not ready for school and the bus will be here in five minutes. Did you hear that boys, get a move on or you are gonna miss the bus. Let's hustle." Turning back to the phone I said "Let's get together tomorrow." I grab the oatmeal bowls off the table so I can get them in the dishwasher before we leave. Nothing out of place. "I really have to go, sister. Boys, now!"

I can't let the boys miss the bus. Scott hates when I don't have control in the morning. It's kindergarten for God's sake, not college. One or two missed buses will not shape who they are, but Scott thinks differently. He thinks differently about a lot of things.

Thank God for bluetooth technology. I'm trying to wrestle my five year old twins into shoes and socks when all they really want to do is knock each other, and me, over the head with the foam swords Jeanie brought over last night. "Sam, Max, shoes, now! I don't want to say it again or you will lose Lego time after school."

"Jules, I was hoping we could visit for a bit before Jeanie gets her results. Then, if it's good news we can all celebrate together. Please come over, I'll put on a pot of coffee."

"I'll let you know, I really have to go, dammit, there goes the bus. I'll call you later. Love you." I hung up, cutting Janie off in mid-sentence. Given the chance, she would keep me on the phone all morning. Janie seemed to live in a different reality. No schedules, no planning, just always in the moment.

"Sam, Max, coats and backpacks! Now, we need to go. Hustle, hustle, hustle!" My boys, wonderful, noisy, messy, crazy boys, who make me feel like I need four more arms, finally head out the front door, jackets slung over their shoulders, dragging backpacks. If their father saw this he would be appalled, remind me that I am the adult, not the boys and that I better get things under control. I hate that everything the boys do I see through the filter of whether or not Scott would approve.

I was so excited when I found out I was having twins. Scott and I had decided two, maybe three children was it for us. By the time I got pregnant I wasn't sure I wanted any, so twins worked perfectly. Once and done, no need for multiple pregnancies. We had our two kids, I didn't see the need for a third.

Also, my mother always said how easy Jeanie and I were being so close in age, we always had a built in playmate. When Janie came along, Momma said she was twice the work. I don't know how she would have known since Janie was the invisible person to Momma up until she died.

My beautiful, bratty sister. Janie looked just like Momma, she had gorgeous red hair and the most piercing hazel eyes, but she was a handful. Personally I think Janie was born lonely and had spent her life trying to get someone, anyone's attention. Today is a perfect example of that, Jeanie needed me, she needed both of us, but as usual, Janie has forgotten.

I love both of my sisters but Janie wears me out. She is always so needy, it seems almost like she tries to create drama to get our attention. As if having four kids in four years wasn't enough drama and chaos.

I glance in the rear view mirror and notice that both boys' faces are covered with cinnamon and sugar, this week's breakfast of choice is cinnamon toast. Their father insists they have oatmeal for breakfast every day. Scott says they need something substantial before school. I do make oatmeal, every day, they just won't eat it so I make them what they will eat. "Hey guys," I say, pulling baby wipes out of the box in the console and handing them over the seat back. "Face check, looking pretty gritty back there."

I pull up in front of the school and hop out to make sure they are clean and I hear Sam start to whine. Sweet Sammy, he is my sensitive child, and you can always tell when things aren't making him happy, the whine starts before the words. "What's up Sam?" I'm trying to be businesslike, sometimes that will head off the tears.

"Mommy, we forgot my show and tell." His bottom lip is starting to quiver.

"No we didn't Buddy, we put it in your backpack right after school yesterday, remember?"

"Let me look Sam," Max said, "I'll help you find it." Max appointed himself his brother's keeper almost immediately after birth. Max is happy, laughing and adventurous, but his sweetest trait is being able to understand his brother and make him happy when no one else can.

"No Max, I want my sword for show and tell, it won't fit in my backpack." Sam is really pouting now, the whine almost drowns out the words.

"Sam, look at me," I'm standing next to the open car door. "We talked about this last night, a sword is a weapon and even though it's a play sword, Daddy and I don't think it's appropriate for show and tell. Remember what we said- nothing that could be considered dangerous can come to school."

“But Mommy, it's soft, and I would never hit anyone with it.” This from the boy who whacked me at least five times just this morning. Those big brown eyes threaten to melt my heart. “Please, please, please?”

“No Sam, no sword, not today, not tomorrow, not ever. You need to remember the rules.” I can’t give in, Scott gets furious when I give in to Sam’s whining. When I see Jeanie she is getting a piece of my mind for this. “Come on, bud, out of the car. The bell is going to ring. Everyone will love the bugs you and Daddy and Max found when you were hiking.”

Sam slumped out of the car, Max started patting his back, soothing and communicating with his brother in their wordless twin speak.

A few feet away Sam turns back to look at me, “The sword is the coolest Mommy. Aunt Jeanie would understand.” The boys quickly ran back and kissed me and then walked over to their friends who were already on the playground.

Aunt Jeanie would understand? Unfortunately, that was the farthest thing from the truth, and one of the reasons my stress level was rising today.

Back in the car, my mind is running over my schedule for the day and trying to figure out how I'm going to get everything done. I need to run a few errands before I go to Jeanie's house. I pull out of the lot and head for the grocery store.

My cell keeps beeping, it's Janie, she is either calling or texting, basically making me crazy. I pull into the parking lot and pick up the phone to call Jeanie. I quickly scroll through Janie's texts to make sure there is nothing life threatening going on. A text from Jeanie pops up, a sad face emoji.

I quickly text back that I'm alone and going to call, I know she won't answer if she thinks there is anyone else with me. I pull out of the parking spot, the grocery store can wait. I give Jeanie a minute, and hit dial.

Jeanie answers, her quiet voice breaking my heart.

"Hey sister, I'm stopping at the store, do you need anything?"

"No, I'm fine." My sister sounds anything but fine.

"Have you eaten?" I know she hasn't and I also know she will lie and say she has.

"Yes, I, ummm, I had some toast, Todd made it for me before he left for work. Is your other line beeping, do you need to take that? Is it the boys?" My sister loves to turn the attention away from herself.

"No, it's not the boys, I just dropped them off at school. I think even heathens like the two of them would need longer than ten minutes to burn the school down. I'm sure it's just Janie, she has been calling all morning. She wants me to come over, said she needs some adult company."

“Please don't bring her here, I don't think I can listen to her today.” Jeanie is crying now. “I just.....can't”

“It's ok, sister, she's not coming over. Just me, with coffee and those cranberry orange scones you love. Gotta go, I'm pulling up to the drive thru, I'm at the one on the corner so I'll be there in a minute. Love you.”

I place our order and my phone rings again. It's Janie, of course it is, it's always Janie.

“Hey sister. “ I say as I answer the phone. “I’m not coming over, I’m going to Jeanie’s, she got bad news again so I'm headed there.” Sometimes the business-like approach works with Janie, too.

“Poor Jeanie, why doesn't she ever ask me to come over when something happens? If you come over, we can have the kids ready to go in no time. Let her spend a little time with my wild ones and she’ll be grateful for a little extra time to herself.”

“Janie, that is exactly why Jeanie doesn't ask you to come over. I know you think you are being sympathetic but when you say things like that, but it just makes her very sad. Jeanie always wonders why other people can have kids, even more kids than they can handle, but she can't and when you say things like that it makes her wonder why you keep having kids.”

“I love my kids! Yes they are wild, crazy, and full of energy but I love my kids, and I deserve to have my babies. I can't believe my own sister would think I don't deserve to have them!” Now Janie is crying, the drama train is rolling. The day just keeps getting better.

“Janie that is not what Jeanie thinks and you know it. She is really hurting. Stop thinking about yourself, this is not about you and your kids, it's about Jeanie. I gotta go, I need to pay for my coffee, love you.” Again, I hang up the phone before Janie can speak.

Our entire lives, Janie has never been able to look at things from my or Jeanie’s point of view, she sees everything through the lens of how it affects her. Even when someone is in crisis, real crisis, not imagined, Janie doesn't see it, or she doesn't want to. As selfish as Janie can be when it comes to her sisters, she is the complete opposite with her husband and children. They are the sun Janie revolves around.

Jeanie and Todd have a cute little cape cod, made even cuter by Jeanie's eye for decorating and Todd's landscaping skills. I park in the driveway, grab our breakfast, and let myself in the house. "Hey sister, I'm here, the scones are still warm, get your butt down the steps."

My baby sister walks into the room, and my heart breaks. Even though she is not the baby, to me, Jeanie is always the baby. Although we are less than a year a part in age, I always feel so much older.

Jeanie and I could be twins. Our features and coloring are almost identical. Brown hair, brown eyes, and our Daddy's nose. The only thing that spoils the twin illusion is that Jeanie is tiny, barely five feet tall while Janie and I are both almost six feet. Thanks, Dad, for the Amazon genes.

I give my sister a hug, and she cries. I let her cry, knowing there is nothing I can say, nothing I can do. Silence is better than the old, tired expressions she hears every time from well-intentioned people.

"It'll be ok sweetie, you'll get through this." Jeanie knows she will get through this, she always does, but it will never be okay, there will always be something missing.

"There's always next time." Every time someone says that I want to kick them. Jeanie has been though this enough to know that the odds next time are no better than they were the last time.

The sobs slow down and I realize that Jeanie and I have our own wordless twin language, just like Sam and Max. I'll tell her about it one day, not today though. The sword discussion will wait for another day as well.

"Sit, let me heat up your coffee and scone and I will tell you what that crazy woman down the street wore to drop off kids today." Jeanie choked out a little laugh, my neighbor always gets her laughing.

I pop the coffee in the microwave. “Ok so Tiffanie LaBell, you know, I still can't help but wonder if she changed her name after the divorce, I mean seriously, Tiffie LaBell? I know it's Tiffanie but she insists we all call her Tiffie. Anyway, I'm prying Sam from the car when out of the corner of my eye I see what looks like walking cotton candy.” I transfer the coffee from the microwave to the table and put the scones in to heat. “I hear- Juleeeeeeeeeaaaaaaaaaa, you know the way she says my name, I swear, no one has called me Julia since Grammy and Pop Pop died, but this woman, she calls me Julia. I look at her and have to look away. I'm not freaking kidding, this woman was a walking pink train wreck! She had on this light pink top, with FEATHERS! Can you believe that? Piles and piles of pink feathers, and the shirt was practically cut to her navel and she was wearing pink skinny jeans and pink thigh high hooker boots! Where does this woman shop? And how in the hell does she take care of those kids? I think her daughter is actually starting to get embarrassed by it, I think she's noticed that none of the other kindergarteners and their moms wear matching outfits.”

"Shut up!" Jeanie is crying again, but this time it's because she is laughing so hard. "That woman did not dress Mercedes in an outfit like that!"

"Well, except for the hooker boots, it's probably hard to find hooker boots for a five year old." The whole story is a lie. I don't know anyone named Tiffanie LaBell, but the first time Jeanie had an unsuccessful IVF cycle and I didn't know what to say I tried to distract her by telling her about the new family in my neighborhood. It works every time. I love to see Jeanie laugh.

"You, sister dear, are going to hell." Jeanie wipes her eyes, "That poor woman is searching for a friend to help her and you keep letting her down. What did she want anyway, Juuuulleeeeeaaaaa?"

"Some fundraiser, probably for kids who can't afford pink feathers and hooker boots. I told her I thought I was coming down with dyfocus of the blowhole and that it might be contagious, she backed off pretty quick."

“You did not! No one would believe that. Well, I guess Tiffie would.” Jeanie got quiet, “Todd doesn't want to try again. He reminded me before we started that this was the last time. We agreed to three cycles before trying another route, but I’m not ready to give up.”

“I'm sorry sis, I can't imagine how hard this is, maybe you need a little break. That might put things in perspective, you may decide you are ready to pursue another route or Todd may want to try again. It’s hard on both of you, a break might be what you need.”

“Yeah, it's so expensive. It's all so expensive, no matter what we do. IVF, surrogacy, adoption, everything costs a fortune. And we're running out of time, I'm not getting any younger you know.” Jeanie gave one of those weak little smiles.

“So what's next sister? What options are you considering at this point? Not Todd, you.”

Jeanie let out a huge sigh, “Surrogacy is our next best option. We still have six frozen embryos so we can have a biological child, we just need to find a surrogate. The thought of someone I don't know carrying my baby though, it kind of freaks me out. How do I know she will take care of it? What if she smokes, or drinks or worse? What if she doesn't care about the baby, just the money?"

"I don't think anyone would go through pregnancy, labor and delivery, just for the money. I'm sure the agency screens those women pretty well."

"Realistically I know that, I just don't think I'm ready to give up on carrying my own child. Does that make me selfish?" Jeanie's brown eyes, looking so much like Sam's this morning, "I think, if we chose another route Todd could be a Dad, am I keeping him from that because I'm selfish? After all, I'm the one who's broken, not him."

"Sister, you are not broken and Todd would be upset if he heard you refer to yourself that way. I know that Todd would rather have you, healthy and happy, than one hundred kids. Give yourself a break, be nice to yourself. The two of you will figure out what's next for your family, you don’t have to decide today.” I felt horrible. I had no problem getting pregnant. In fact, I tried to avoid it.

I left Jeanie's and headed to Janie's, if I didn't at least stop in there I would never hear the end of it. Janie loves to say how no one takes her seriously and no one is ever there for her when she needs them, how she feels all alone in the world. Janie is twenty-nine but most of the time acts like she's thirteen. I thought she would outgrow this, I thought this behavior was just from being the baby. I thought when her own babies started coming she would change. I was wrong. It was, and still is, all about Janie.

The kids saw me pull up and tumbled out of the house like puppies. Collin, the oldest at 4 was at the car almost before it stopped. I got out of the car and Collin attacked me with his foam sword. “You dead, Aunt Julie, you dead. I got you.”

“Good thing I put on my sword proof vest this morning. Aunt Jeanie bought me one because she knew all you boys would get me with those swords. Now give me a hug.”

Collin barreled at me, followed by Lacey and Brie, who attacked my legs. At just eighteen months Brie was a wobbly little thing, running on her stubby legs, very much like her mother had been at the same age. I kissed Collin and Lacey and scooped Brie up. "Where's your Momma, Collin?"

"She's feeding the baby, he cries all the time. Daddy said if that baby didn't stop crying he was gonna start sleeping in his car. You think Daddy would really do that, Aunt Julie?" I laughed at Collin's serious little expression.

"Oh baby boy, we all said that when every one of you was a baby. Me and your Momma, our babies just cry a lot. When I was a little girl and your Aunt Neenie was a baby, she cried all the time, I used to call her a crybaby, but my Pop told me that some babies don't know about happiness and that if we are bigger we need to teach them to be happy. Look how well it worked! You and Lacey and Brie are happy all the time. You just have to teach Porter about happiness, then he won't cry so much."

Janie heard me come in. “Jules, if you can teach this one to be happy, I'll be grateful forever. I don't remember any of the others crying this much, or maybe I'm just more tired with him. Poor little guy, getting such a tired out Momma.”

“Bryan still out of town?” I asked, picking up my littlest nephew and snuggling him against my chest.

“Yes, he's coming home tonight. I told him he needs to be home more, I can't do this by myself. I feel like I haven't had a shower in days.”

“Go, take a shower, I have an hour before I have to leave to be home for the boys. Shower, fix your hair, whatever, I'll play with the kids.”

“You are the best, sister. I can always count on you. Maybe I'll take a bubble bath and read a book, I never get to do that anymore.” Janie was already headed down the hall, visions of quiet time dancing in her head.

I looked around the house. My littlest sister is a whirlwind with the attention span of a gnat. Looking around the kitchen and family room I can see the projects she started before getting distracted by something else.

I put the baby in a sling and got the toddlers to play clean up games with me so that by the time my sister was out of the bath we had the family room and kitchen picked up and the kids were drawing pictures at the kitchen table.

"I feel wonderful. I needed that, thanks sister." Janie came into the kitchen, her hair still wrapped in a towel. "Do you guys have any plans for tonight?"

"No plans, I need to get some writing done tonight after Scott gets home, so he'll probably take the kids to the park while I work. What are you doing?" That wasn't the truth, I could never write when Scott was home, but I knew Janie wanted something.

Janie let out her weight of the world sigh, “Well, Bryan comes home and I wanted to have an evening alone with him. Do you think you could take the kids overnight?”

“I can take Collin, Janie, but if I take the girls and the baby I won't get anything done.” The truth was Scott would be furious, he already thought I didn’t get enough done at home. The noise and mess of all of Janie’s kids would push him over the edge and make for a very rough week for me and my boys.

“Fine, it was just a thought. Don't take Collin, he helps me with the girls so if you can't take them then leave him home.” Unfortunately Collin heard this exchange.

“I wanna go to Aunt Julie's and play with Max and Sam, I don't wanna play with the girls anymore. I don't like sisters, I only like brothers.” Collin put on his best mad, pouty face, it was all I could do not to laugh at him.

“Not this time baby boy, Momma needs your help, maybe next time.”

“No fair! I wanna go!” With that Collin started crying. Janie looked at me as if to say ‘look what you started.’

“I'll call Jeanie and see if she will take the girls.” Janie said, picking up her cell phone.

“Are you freaking kidding me? Come on Janie, after what she just went through you are going to call her and ask her to keep your kids? What are you thinking?” I took the phone out of her hand. “Come on Janie, try and consider Jeanie's feelings, just this once.”

“I get so tired of hearing that, think about Jeanie, look at everything Jeanie has to go through, poor Jeanie. What about me? Everyone acts like just because my sister can't have kids I should never ask for help with mine. Well guess what, big sister, we are not all perfect and organized like you! I just wanted to be able to tell Bryan….” Janie stomped out of the kitchen.

"Tell Bryan what sister? Are you pregnant again?" I don't know why it surprised me but it does.

"Yes, I just found out yesterday. Stop looking at me like that, yes I know what causes this and believe it or not sister, all of my babies are planned."

"You planned this? Janie, how could you be so insensitive, you knew Jeanie was trying again, why didn't you wait?" I cannot believe my sister, she knows how much Jeanie wants a baby and now, so soon after another failed cycle, Janie is pregnant.

"Yes, I planned this. I thought, well, I guess I thought Jeanie and I could be pregnant together. I'm sorry it didn't work for her but does that mean everyone needs to act like I shouldn't have another baby? Where is the joy for this little one?" Janie is crying again.

"Sister, you know we are all happy about your babies, it's just not the best timing. Please don't tell Jeanie yet, give her some time to grieve. You know she will be excited about a new baby, just give her time, ok?"

"I won't say anything," Janie took Porter from me and snuggled him, "No wonder you have such a tired Momma little guy."

"I have to run. I'll call you tomorrow." I did not have the energy or patience to deal with my baby sister today.

Time for other options

"Do you want to go out to eat tonight?" Todd asked after he kissed me hello, "I think a little dinner and a mindless comedy would be good for us."

"No, I want to stay in, I'm sorry I didn't even think about dinner, I can call and order Chinese." I pulled the blanket back up to my neck. I was grateful the test results came back early, it's hard to wait half the day and then be disappointed. Better to get it over early and let the mourning begin.

The days after a negative test are the worst. I still have to go to work, mourning something that never existed is not a legitimate excuse for missing work. So, I'll go in, smile, make small talk, do my job, mostly with the office door closed, and clock out as soon as I can. Fortunately, most of what I do is behind the scenes so any communication can be done over email. There is rarely anything urgent enough for someone to disturb me.

The first time we tried IVF I told a few women in the office. I was so excited, sure that it was going to work, I never thought about what would happen if it didn't. That time, my period came before I even went for the bloodwork. A coworker found me crying in the bathroom and in record time the news that I was not pregnant was all over the office. I went home early that day and then called in the next two days. That was the last time I told anyone other than my sisters.

I'm not sure which is harder, no one knowing or everyone knowing. Either way, I just want to stay home and wallow in self-pity.

"Let's go out, laugh a little, try to have some fun. This is hard sweetie, so hard, but at least now we can move on." Todd was trying to pull me out of myself, but I didn't want to hear it.

"I'm not sure I'm ready to move on and I don't want to talk about it right now." I looked away, back to the game show that I had been watching when he came in.

“We don’t have to talk about it tonight, but we did agree, this was the last. I can’t watch you go through this over and over, it’s too hard”

“It’s too hard? Too hard for you to watch? Are you kidding me? You are not the one going through anything. I’m the one stuck full of needles and weird probes and endless doctors appointments, just to find out- hey, you are broken after all.” I was crying again. I’m always crying and always taking it out on Todd.

“Ok, let’s not talk, there’s plenty of time for that. You are not broken, Jeanie, please don’t say that. This is what was meant to be for us. It’s hard, but we’ll get through it. What are you watching? Didn’t this show go off the air a couple years ago?” Todd was trying to change the subject and I was grateful.

“I wondered why that guy was on here, didn’t he die last year? Oh man, I really am pathetic. I’m sorry Todd,” I hugged my husband, “I know this is hard for you too. I’m just feeling sorry for myself. So how about Chinese?”

“Chinese it is. I’ll call. Let me change first.” Todd went upstairs to change out of his work clothes.

I got up to at least wash my face. That’s when I got my period. Stupid body. Even though I know I’m not pregnant that first drop of blood is still a slap in the face. Why, oh, why can’t this be easier for us? Todd would be such an amazing father. I can hear him coming back downstairs and try to pull myself together again.

“I called in dinner, it will be about 45 minutes. Do you want to try to find a movie? Or should we just keep watching a dead man host a game show?” Todd was trying to be funny, but I wasn’t in the mood.

“I think I want to go to bed early tonight. I’m beat. We can watch something in bed if you want.”

Todd came up behind me and wrapped me in his arms, “Do you want to talk? The doctor said that it helps to talk, not to keep things bottled up. We don’t have to talk about what’s next, just right now, what you are feeling.”

I looked at him, knowing he wanted to talk, to hear that I'm okay, that I'm ready for the next steps but I can't do it. I can't say the things he wants to hear. "I'm sorry. This time seems so much harder. Maybe it's all that 'third time's the charm' bullshit. I really thought it would work this time. It seemed only fair."

My shoulders were shaking from crying again and Todd turned me around to face him. "I know, it seems harder to me, too. I just don't know what we could have done differently. I don't know... well, I don't know anything and that is so frustrating."

We stood in the hallway, Todd holding me while I cried. Several times he started to speak, but stopped. There really isn't anything to say. My body just keeps rejecting our babies and no one can tell us why.

A knock at the door startled us. I glanced at the clock in the kitchen, had I really been crying for over half an hour?

I set the table while Todd paid the delivery guy. I lit the candles in the middle of the table. I didn't have a baby but I still had Todd and sometimes that seemed like the only thing I had going for me.

Todd tried to make conversation all through dinner but my mind wasn't on what he was saying. I was trying to think of a way to convince him to try again. Just one more time. Yes, this sucks but I'm not ready to give up. I want to carry my own baby. I want to feel it kick and get heartburn and stretch marks and maybe pee my pants. All the wonderful, glorious, messy, and inconvenient parts of being pregnant. I want those, for me, not someone else. How can I make Todd understand?

"Well, since my witty banter is not lightening the mood, let's go back to your game show." Todd said, getting up to clear the table.

I appreciate so much how hard he tries. I do want to talk about what's next, but not surrogates or adoption or anything else. I want to carry our baby. I stand up and push in my chair. "I'm not doing a surrogate, not yet. I don't feel ready to give up."

“Sweetie, we agreed” Todd started.

“Yes, we agreed, I would agree to anything when I thought this time would work. I didn’t think there would be a need for a surrogate, I thought this time would be different. I cannot stand the thought of our child growing in someone else’s body. Some stranger knowing our child before I do. Feeling all of the things that I want to feel. I may never be ready for that.” I turned and went upstairs, not caring if Todd followed or what he had to say.

Later I wake up when Todd comes to bed but I don't let him know I'm awake. I still don't want to talk to him. How can he be so stubborn about this? How can he think its okay for someone else to carry our baby, I just don't understand.

Todd gets into bed and puts his arm around me. I lay still with my back turned to him, I feel him breathing against my ear and know he wants to say something. I still pretend I'm asleep.

"Jeanie, we agreed, three was the number of times we were willing to try IVF before moving on. I know you didn't think it would turn out this way but we did agree. We talked about this at length, planned for every possibility. We still have the frozen embryos and I think our best chance, at this point, is to have a surrogate carry them. Later we can try again with IVF, if that's what you want to do but I know how badly you want to be a mom. All of these unsuccessful cycles, they're taking a toll on you. You need to give your body a rest and let someone else do this for us."

I didn't answer and he rolled away. I laid awake for hours trying to imagine what it would be like to have someone else tell me that my baby kicked today or that he or she has the hiccups. I just don't think I can do it. Those experiences should be mine.

I've tried thinking about surrogacy, just trying to focus on the end result but it still feels like a kick in the gut. Someone else giving my husband the child he wants because I can't. I've tried to think of a scenario where I would really be okay with surrogacy and lately I've thought that maybe if one of my sisters were to be my surrogate, I could handle it. At least then I could be intimately involved. I don't want to be a stranger to the person who carries our baby.

I've tried to think how I could bring it up with Janie or Julie. I wouldn't even know how to ask. Janie is always pregnant, I'm not sure when she could fit in a baby for me and Julie, well, Julie's life is so regimented and scheduled, I'm just not sure she could relax her super mom mode long enough to be pregnant again. Why can't this be easier? Why does everything have to be planned and paid for. Why can't I be like Janie?

Keep those babies coming

I watch my sister back out of the driveway and turn around and head into the living room, back to my babies. I don't know why my sisters can't be happy for me, look at my beautiful children. Do they think I don't know how lucky I am to have each and every one of them, do they think I don't know anything about infertility? I was so surprised that Jeanie was the one with infertility problems. I had been sure it was going to going to be me.

When I was 16 I went to a party and I had sex with a boy while I was there. I spent so much of my life looking for someone to love me and I thought that maybe that would do it. Well of course it didn't all it did was freak me out that I was going to be pregnant and my sisters were going to kill me. I spent the next several weeks just praying, praying to God that I would get my period. I promised God that if I wasn't pregnant I would never do anything stupid again as long as I live. I paced the floor of my room and ranted about all the reasons that I didn't need a baby. I couldn't have a baby, I wasn't going to have a baby. Thankfully, I wasn't pregnant, I didn't ruin my life over a stupid boy at a party. The night I got my period Julie found me crying in my room. I was so relieved, all I could do was cry and say thank you, over and over.

When Julie found me crying she thought something was wrong. My big sister really fell hard into the mom role and she kept asking, over and over what was wrong until I finally told her about the party and about the boy. Julie was ready to have him arrested. She was sure that I had been raped and this was against my will. Even if it wasn't, she wanted him arrested because I was too young to consent.

I kept telling her no, but in typical Julie fashion, she didn't listen. When my sister makes up her mind about something, she is going to see it through no matter what. It wasn't until I finally said I wanted to do it that she listened. Julie got up off my bed, walked out of my room, and shut the door quietly behind her.

I knew she was disappointed but there wasn't anything I could do about it now. A few days later I saw on the calendar “Janie PP appt”. I asked Julie what it was she said it was a Planned Parenthood appointment.

I was mad at her but I was also relieved, now I wouldn’t have to worry anymore. I went to the appointment, got put on the pill, and the next couple years I kept looking for someone to love. I wasn't always good about taking the pill. I would forget, for days at a time, then I'd meet someone and I would start taking them again.

Somehow I got lucky and nothing ever happened. I have friends who missed one pill, or took an antibiotic, and got pregnant. I never had so much as a scare. I kept telling myself that I was lucky, nothing bad was going to happen.

Then I met Bryan. I was 22 when I met him and as silly as it sounds, as soon as I met him I knew that he was my home, he was my forever. I went and got an IUD inserted because we weren't going to have children until after we were married.

In the back of my mind, I kept thinking that maybe God listened a little too well when I begged not to be pregnant. Maybe because of that mistake when I was 16, maybe God wasn't going to let me have kids. I knew the way that I messed around with my pills, I should have gotten pregnant. I should have gotten pregnant multiple times, but it didn't happen.

When Bryan and I started talking about the future and our family, I was afraid it would never happen, that I had broken something by not wanting to be pregnant. I started studying infertility. The causes, symptoms, what you can do if you are infertile. I studied everything I could get my hands on. I knew that there was something wrong with me and I wasn't going to be able to have children.

After the wedding, we waited a year before deciding we were ready for a family. I had all my fingers and all my toes crossed. I really and truly had convinced myself that because of my past transgressions I was going to be infertile. Those first two months and the negative pregnancy test were the hardest things I ever went through.

When I got pregnant with Collin, I was over the moon. And each pregnancy since then has been just as miraculous and just as exciting to me. Why can't my sisters understand that? Why can't they be happy for me?

I know that Jeanie is going through a lot, but that doesn't take the joy away from my children. This baby is just as loved and wanted as my other four. If my sisters don't want to be a part of that and they can't be excited for us, then they don't need to be around my children. I don't ever want my children to think that they're not special, that they're not wanted. I spent enough of my own life with that hanging over my head, I won't allow anyone to make my babies feel the way I did.

The kids and I played with their new toys all afternoon. I didn't realize the day had passed until I heard Bryan's voice booming through the house, "What? No one wants to say hi to their father? Where are my children? Where is my wife?" Bryan was smiling when he came into the family room. "Looks like Aunt Jeanie has been here and now you are all dressed the part as members of my kingdom." Bryan came over and gave me a kiss before scooping up Brie and untangling her from her wig. "Any thoughts about dinner? I'm starving."

"Sorry babe, we have been terribly busy slaying dragons while you were away." The kids all giggled that mom and dad were playing along.

"No problem, as the king, I shall make a feast to feed my family." Bryan headed off to the kitchen to make his specialty, spaghetti with a mountain of mozzarella cheese melted over it. I felt my throat constrict. When I'm pregnant the only thing that bothers me is melted cheese. The thought of Bryan's spaghetti made it hard to keep my lunch down.

"No cheese for me" I called to the kitchen.

Bryan poked his head into the family room, "Something you want to tell me?" He asked with a smile.

"Nothing you don't already know." I said. So much for finding a sweet, romantic way to tell him that number five was on the way.

Bryan crossed the room and gave me a big hug. At least my husband is happy about our baby. “Have you told everyone, do the kids know?” Bryan asked.

I sighed, “Julie knows, and she is not thrilled. Jeanie got another negative test, so now I’m selfish. As much as I hate not being able to celebrate this baby, we have to keep it under wraps until Jeanie is feeling better. Julie seems to think I get pregnant just to rub in Jeanie’s nose that I can. I really thought it would work for her this time and our babies could be super close.” I lean into Bryan and close my eyes. I am so tired of my sisters making me feel like my family is less important just because it comes so easily to us.

“Babe, it’s just bad timing. I know you had good intentions and your sisters will too, once they come around. You know Julie and Jeanie both will be so excited. They love our littles and each time a new one comes along they are thrilled. Give Jeanie a week or two and she will be asking when the next little one is going to be here.”

"I know you are right. I just felt so judged today by Julie. I mean, she's always judgmental, that's who she is, but today she seemed super judgy about my life choices. Maybe I'm just tired, this little guy really seems to be sapping all of my energy." I flopped on the couch as if to illustrate my point.

"Little guy? Is that what you're thinking?" Bryan asked with a smile, "They say Momma knows, but for the record, you have been wrong 50% of the time."

I tossed a pillow from the couch at him. "Beats your one out of four!" I started laughing. Whatever intuition it is that makes mothers seem to know what their babies will be, I don't have it. I wanted a boy so badly with Collin, but it was a lucky guess and then after two girls I was so ready for a boy that Porter was a lucky guess as well. I guessed boy every time I was pregnant. For some reason, it was my go to and my guess now was boy as well.

Bryan was right about Lacey, he said he knew she was a girl the minute the test was positive. Since we never find out until they are here,

Lacey would have come home in one of Collin's hand me downs if my sisters hadn't saved the day and bought every pink thing they could find.

Bryan headed back into the kitchen to finish dinner. I looked at my littles playing happily together and decided that this is the best life. I won't hurt Jeanie but I won't hide my excitement when she's not around.

Porter came over to be picked up and I actually fell asleep snuggling him. Bryan woke me up for dinner and then let me go to bed. I was exhausted. My last thought before falling asleep was about how good my life is and how lucky I am to have someone like Bryan to share in every moment.

Scott is in charge

Even without bringing Janie's kids home with me, the boys and I had a rough week. Make that a rough couple of weeks.

Scott's company was opening a new branch in another state and Scott's boss told him he was in charge of opening the branch, doing all the hiring, ordering office equipment and supplies. Basically, setting everything up. So a month after Janie found out she was pregnant and Jeanie found out she wasn't, Scott was going to be out of state for three weeks out of every month until everything was set up at the new location.

Scott was on a mission to get us all in line before he had to leave. All that meant was that no matter what we did, it was never good enough. Scott told me night after night how the boys we going to be juvenile delinquents because I was such a shitty mother. This certainly isn’t the life I expected.

Growing up, I couldn't wait to be a wife and mother, to correct all the things that were wrong with my childhood and give my kids something better. Then I got married.

Marriage is not at all what I expected. Scott is not at all what I expected. He is controlling, manipulative, and mean; just not so that anyone can see. The signs were there when we were dating. Looking back now, I can see them, but I chose to ignore them because he said he loved me and painted a beautiful picture of what our life would be like. I should have paid more attention to his actions than his words. I have learned that people can say anything, it is how they behave that tells the truth.

My sisters tease me about being a drill sergeant and being too organized and never having any fun. What they don't know is that Scott is the drill sergeant, and if my house is not run the way he expects there is hell to pay. He's never hit me, and he is wonderful to the boys, but in one sentence he can destroy any sense of self-esteem or success I feel.

When we were first married I learned that Scott expected things a certain way, everything from how the towels were folded to what cabinet we used for the coffee cups. In the beginning I was happy to do what made him happy, it didn't seem like a big deal, and he always made me feel so guilty when things weren't how he wanted them, like I was purposely trying to make him unhappy. So I tried harder.

By the time he decided we were ready to have children I was pretty sure I never wanted kids, I didn't even really want to be married anymore. I didn't have anyone to talk to because Scott was always sweet, friendly, and kind when we were around my sisters. It was just when we were alone that he would brow beat me about everything I said, everything I did, why couldn't I do......whatever it was that day that he had decided was wrong with me.

I pretended to be excited about getting pregnant, when really it was my worst nightmare. I continued to take my birth control faithfully, even going to Planned Parenthood to get it so it wouldn't show on our prescription benefit. I got away with this for about a year, then Scott got concerned and wanted to go to the doctor to see what was wrong with me, I would remind him of the friends we had who had taken a while to get pregnant and now had several children. After that year, I had to throw away the birth control.

I tried so hard to not get pregnant, I kept hoping that because I was on the pill for so long that would delay it even more but I got pregnant immediately. I cried and cried and cried. Scott was beaming. He was going to be a Daddy, and he couldn't wait to tell our families, to let everyone know that we were going to have a baby. I hated my body and the baby in it, they both had let me down.

In the beginning Scott was wonderful, I thought that maybe this was what we needed all along, that having children would change him. When we found out we were having twins, he brought me flowers, he took me to dinner, he pampered me. It was wonderful. Then sometime around my sixth month, that all changed.

Suddenly, I wasn't doing anything right. I was sitting too much, which was going to make my labor hard and increase the possibility that I would have a c-section, or so Scott said. I wasn't eating the right things, or enough of them. I was gaining too much weight. I wasn't resting enough, I was resting too much. The nursery wasn't done, what did I do with all my time?

After a week or two of that I realized that nothing had changed or would change, and knew that I better get with the program. I had initially worked at a job I loved but after six months of trying with no success Scott had decided it was the stress from my job that was keeping me from getting pregnant so I had given my notice. We decided I would stay home once we had kids, Scott made more than enough money to support our family. I would stay home and make a home and raise our children. Now, I was going to have two kids. There was no longer a light at the end of the tunnel.

So, I got with the program. I spent the rest of my pregnancy completely organizing and baby proofing the house, according to Scott's instructions. I finished the nursery, folded all the little clothes, sheets, and towels we had bought. I lived my life according to the schedule Scott set for me.

When the boys were born, just like when I got pregnant, initially, things were wonderful. Scott was attentive and loving with me and he adored the boys. He got up in the middle of the night and brought them to me for feedings. We snuggled while the boys ate, just in awe of them.

When the boys were three months old, the old Scott came back. Why aren't they sleeping through the night? Why does Sam cry so much? Don't leave Max in his infant seat to hold Sam, let him cry it out. Make them stop crying. The house stinks like baby puke. Why didn't you empty the diaper pail, didn't you get any laundry done today? What do you do with your time?

For three months I got to enjoy my boys. When they cried, I held them. When they were hungry, I fed them. When they were happy, I played with them. When they napped, I napped. All too soon Scott decided that the reason the babies weren't on any schedule was because I was lazy and unorganized, so he put together a schedule for me. Every minute of every day was scheduled. The boys ate, slept, and played according to schedule.

My house ran like a boot camp, because Scott said so. Forget sleeping in, even if the boys did sleep past seven, which was when Scott thought they should eat, I would have to wake them up so they didn't throw the rest of the days schedule off. It took about a month, but the boys adjusted, and so did I. That's when my sisters really started teasing me.

My schedule was made using a computer program and every Sunday we sat down to tweak it based on what was scheduled that week that was outside the norm, like doctors' appointments, dinners with friends, lunch with his mother, things like that. God forbid I didn't adhere to that schedule. If the pediatrician was running late and I got home later than expected and dinner wasn't ready, or the boys were taking a late nap, or the laundry wasn't folded, I got a lecture.

Scott told me so many times that I needed to take some initiative and think for myself, that he couldn't always tell me how to use my time.

That was a laugh. Any time I would do something my way instead of his, it wasn't the right thing and he would let me know what I should have done instead.

Yes, life is good, what a laugh. My sisters think my life is perfect. Around other people, Scott is wonderful, kind, loving even; but as soon as we are alone he lets me know everything that I did wrong while we were with other people.

My sisters are amazed at how well I'm able to do everything, how devoted I am to my husband and children. What would they think if they knew how much I hate my husband, how much I resent my boys for being born and trapping me in this marriage, how much I wish I could just walk away?

I thought the weeks leading up to Scott's first trip back east were the worst, but I was wrong. When Scott was out of town, somehow, he was even more demanding. He was convinced that I would ruin the boys while he was away. Every night we went over all the rules, the things I needed to accomplish the next day. What the boys had eaten, if they did their chores, how their day was at school. Then I had to walk him through the house so he could see that we hadn't managed to destroy it while he was gone.

No matter how carefully I went through the house before those Skype calls, Scott would find something wrong. The lid to the hamper was up, the boys shoes weren't lined up neatly by the door, something. If nothing was wrong, Scott was sure it was because I was focusing too much on the house and neglecting the boys. I could not win.

Every night we went over the entire day, if I said the boys didn't do anything naughty, Scott accused me of lying to cover up for myself, my lack of parenting skills. I quickly found that he could turn the smallest thing against me, like the time I was telling him what I thought was a funny story about the boys, but I made the mistake of saying that Max knocked Sam down getting out of the van because he was so excited. That little slip resulted in an hour long lecture about how out of control Max was now that he was out of town. I became afraid to tell him anything. It killed Scott not to be home and be in control.

My saving grace was my blog. I had started it after the boys were born, mostly as a way to remember everything. There's so many little things that happen every day that you forget. I thought a blog would be a perfect way to remember all those things, like how Max would grunt when he cried and how Sam hated being on his tummy. It started as just a baby book for the boys, I wasn't looking to do anything with it.

To my surprise people started following it, other twin moms, moms of singletons who thought it would be fun to have twins. People started following and commenting, it was fun, I felt like I had a little community of friends. After a while I had a good little following and I showed it to Scott of course he thought it was a waste of time.

I had read other bloggers were able to make some money with their blogs so I put some ads on my blog and the very first month I made $3.27. I was so excited when Scott came home but he just laughed at me and asked if I knew how many years it would take me to make what he made a month.

A tiny little fire was lit, maybe there was a light at the end of the tunnel after all. When I got my next check I opened a savings account, in my name only. I told Scott it was for the boys, for college. I always let Scott know how much money the blog was making and fortunately for me Scott was proud and arrogant and no wife of his was going to be paying his bills. As long as I wasn't spending the money he didn't really care what I did with it, he wanted to be able to hold the reins on all the money in our family. So I kept putting the money into that account and it just kept growing.

My blog saved my sanity many times. Of course, I couldn't blog about Scott. I pretended we were the perfect family. If he ever read it I didn't want there to be anything he could hold against me.

Scott traveling was a bonus for my blog. I was able to put more time into it, and even started writing content for other blogs.

Now that Scott has been traveling for a few months, we've settled into a routine. For three weeks out of the month I can breathe, but that one week a month... well, it seems longer than the other three put together. Tonight, Scott was coming home for a week. Jeanie had wanted to meet for lunch but I have too much to do before tonight.

“Mommy, Mommy, Max took my truck and won't give it back, he knows it's my favorite.” Sam came running into the kitchen, crying. I looked at the clock, thirty minutes until the boys’ naptime.

“That was not very nice of Max to take something that is your favorite but the toys belong to both of you and you need to share them all. It's time to clean up for lunch.” I leaned down and gave Sam a quick cuddle and then we headed to the playroom.

“Time to pick up, I'm going to make lunch, I'll set the timer for fifteen minutes.” As I walked out of the room the boys were already putting toys away. Even the playroom was organized according to Scott's standards and my boys had learned long ago not to argue with me and to do what they are told. Scott was wonderful with the boys, I was the one that had to make them toe the line, otherwise I would hear what an absolutely horrible mother I was.

Today's lunch is grilled cheese and tomato soup, we even ate according to Scott's menu. When I spent the day with my sister I felt so bad when she actually asked all of the kids what they wanted for lunch, and made whatever each child wanted. That never happened in our house, once in a while the boys would ask for something different than what I was making but, according to my wonderful husband, this is not a fast food joint and the kids will eat what you put in front of them or they will be hungry.

I knew Max wasn't going to be happy, he is a meat eater, and would want a ham sandwich and then pout because he couldn’t have one. He would eat his lunch anyway because he knew Mom's rule, “You eat what you get and you don't throw a fit.” My boys were good little recruits. It only takes going hungry until snack time once or twice for them to learn that Mom means business.

It made me so sad when the boys wouldn't eat their dinner because it was something they hated and I put them to bed hungry.

Those times were especially hard because Scott made it look like it was all my fault. When the boys would plead with their Dad to let them have a peanut butter and jelly sandwich because they hated meatloaf, he would sympathize but remind them that Mommy made the meals so we have to eat what she makes. I hated him so badly at those times. Our dinner menu was always Scott's decision.

A few seconds before the timer went off both boys were in their chairs, the playroom was clean and their hands were washed. I know that structure is good for kids but just once I would like to let them make a mess, be boys, get dirty and not have to worry about what Scott would say.

I put their lunches in front of them and poured some milk into two glasses. Max made a face but said nothing. With a sigh he picked up his sandwich and took a bite. I grabbed my lunch and sat at the table with the boys. We ate all meals, together, around the table, so we could keep the lines of communication open with the boys so that when they are teenagers they will talk to us about things. Whatever, they are five, they don't care if I sit down with them or not and today I wasn't hungry but I picked at my lunch anyway.

“Thank you for doing such a great job on the playroom. You two are the best helpers I know.”

The boys smiled and Max said, “Sammy didn't help much, he was playing with my truck.”

“Max, finish chewing before you speak, it's rude to talk with your mouth full.” I knew how to recite all the rules to the boys to make sure they behave in a way that was acceptable to their father. “I know that sometimes if feels like one of you does all the work, that's how everyone feels, but you guys do a good job of helping each other. We have to remember to appreciate what someone does instead of complaining about what they don't do.” Yet another behavior expectation, the boys could not tattle on each other.

We talked about what was planned for the rest of the day and how excited we were that Daddy would be home tonight, finished our lunches and the boys went down for their naps. They still shared a room and probably always would. Scott didn't see the need for them to have separate rooms, he was still hoping for a third child. I was not about to let that happen.

Is divorce the answer

Is my marriage falling apart? Is this really going to be the end of us? There have been so many arguments, and both Todd and I are standing our ground. I cannot discuss surrogacy, I just can't. I don't know what could possibly make me change my mind. There is an ache inside of me to just try one more time.

Todd is just as insistent that we're not doing another round of IVF. He says that it takes too much of a toll on me, on our relationship, and that we need to go with something that's more of a sure thing. It was like a slap in the face to hear him say that, a sure thing. I'm no longer a sure thing. I am the one who is supposed to carry his children.

Most nights we barely talk. We come home from work, eat dinner, one or both of us will mention something that happened at work, something funny someone said or that we read. And then we go our separate ways for the rest of the night.

I usually have my nose buried in a book and Todd flips through the channels on the TV acting like he's trying to find something to watch but what he's really doing is trying to find a way to convince me that surrogacy is what we need to do.

I won't talk about it anymore. I can't talk about it anymore. I'm done with the whole subject. Last night I told him that if I can't carry our babies then maybe we're just not meant to have any. The look on his face devastated me.

I know how badly Todd wants to be a father, and he'll be an amazing father, but I can't do it, I just can't. I don't know what another cycle of IVF would change, I don't even know what I would do if we had another unsuccessful cycle. I feel like the only thing I know is that I want to carry our babies.

I agreed to three cycles because I didn't think there was any way that it wouldn't work. I thought for sure we would be one of those couples on the front of the brochures. It was easy to agree to something that I didn't think would ever happen and now that we're there, I'm kicking myself for ever agreeing to discuss other options.

I left work and headed home. Todd had called to say he would be late, not to hold dinner. I was feeling completely lost and alone. Janie is pregnant again, not that anyone has told me, but I know. Janie is always pregnant. To make my week even better, I got my period at work. Even though we weren't going through a cycle, it was still a bright red reminder of all the things we would never have.

I knew I had to talk to Todd. I had to let him out of this childless marriage. Just because I can't have children doesn't mean that he shouldn't. He'll find someone else and she will give him the family he's always wanted. I just had to be strong. If I cried, he would stay, and I certainly don't want him to stay out of pity. I have to let him go while we still care about each other, before my brokenness colors our entire life.

I let myself into our house and let the dogs out. I love our house. We spent so much time painting and decorating and planning everything, together. We bought this house expecting to fill it up with our children.

Now it's just a carefully decorated museum. The rooms meant for our children sit forgotten, filled with boxes and Christmas decorations instead of toys and stuffed animals. It's time to let it go, let Todd plan the rest of his life.

I played with the dogs for a few minutes and heated up some leftovers. I wasn't really hungry so I scraped my plate in the trash, rinsed it, and put it in the dishwasher.

I was on the couch, staring at the TV when I heard Todd's truck in the driveway.

"Jeanie?" Todd called as he opened the door.

“In the family room.” I said, what a joke that was, this room would never hold a family as long as I was in it.

“Hey, how was your day?” Todd kissed me on the cheek and sat down beside me.

“Good, how was yours?” Mindless nonsense, we never talk about anything anymore.

“Long. I stopped and got take out, did you eat? I’m sure there are enough fries for two.” Todd said pulling his sandwich out of the paper bag.

“I had leftovers. I’m going to take a shower, and then I think we should talk.” I said getting up from the couch.

“Sounds serious. Are you okay?” Todd looked at me with concern.

"I'm fine. We just need to clear the air. I'll be down soon." I headed up the stairs going over in my mind what I would say to him.

I stayed under the spray of hot water as long as I could, willing myself not to cry. Todd would know if I cried in the shower, and I needed to be strong and do the right thing.

I got out of the shower, threw on some pajamas, and headed by downstairs. Todd was now the one staring at the TV.

I came into the family room and stood at the end of the couch. "We can't go on like this. This isn't a life for either one of us." I took a deep breath. "I think… I think we should get a divorce."

Almost before the word was out of my mouth Todd jumped up and came over to me, grabbing my upper arms. "Jeanie, what are you talking about? There is nothing wrong with our life. Whatever is wrong, we can work it out, together."

"No, we can't. What is wrong is that I can't have children and you should be able to find someone who can give you children. I've thought about.."

"What?" Todd interrupted me, "You've thought about what? Turning tail and running when the going gets tough? That's not who we are, we decide things together, we fix things together. We don't run from our problems."

"This isn't our problem," I said, stepping away from him, "This is my problem and you shouldn't be saddled with it. I don't want to spend the rest of my life knowing that I didn't give you the family you wanted. I think this is for the best."

Todd just shook his head. "We promised when we got married we would never take the easy way out and decide to divorce rather than work on our problems. This problem has a solution, you just don't want to do it. Maybe that is just an excuse, maybe you really just don't want me anymore."

Todd turned and headed out of the room, I went after him. "Todd, let's discuss this, it makes sense. We can't go on living like this."

"What I can't do is talk to you when you are like this. I don't know what brought this on but I refuse to talk about it with you. If you want a divorce, then get a divorce, but don't expect me to make this easy on you."

I watched Todd walk up the stairs, struggling not to run after him and tell him I didn't mean it. I love him, but I can't hold him back anymore.

I grabbed a blanket out of the linen closet and headed back to the couch. I couldn't risk lying next to him, I knew I couldn't be that strong.

In the morning I woke up to the sound of Todd making coffee. I staggered up the stairs to brush my teeth and wash my face, hoping we wouldn't talk. If he just takes some time to think about it he will realize that I'm giving him a way out. He should not be stuck with a barren wife when he has so much of his life ahead of him.

I was in our closet choosing what to wear to work when I heard Todd come up behind me. "Jeanie."

I turned around, he was holding a cup of coffee for me. "Thank you." I grabbed the cup and squeezed past him. I put the cup on my dresser and was buttoning my shirt when he spoke again.

"One more time." That's all he said and then he walked out of the room.

One more time? What does that mean? Does he want me to say it again? I finished getting dressed and went downstairs.

I was putting my jacket on when Todd came into the mud room. I looked at him, "I don't know what you want me to say. I think I was pretty clear last night. Go on with your life, I'll be fine. This is my problem, not yours."

I put my purse on my shoulder and grabbed the car keys off the hook. Todd put his hand on my arm. “One more time Jeanie, that’s really all I can do. I know I’m not the one who goes through IVF, but this is hard on me too. I’ll agree to one more cycle, with some pretty stiff stipulations, because I can’t stand the thought that you think there is something wrong with you and that I would choose some other women and children I could have over you. I would choose you every time, with or without children. Now go to work and never say that word to me again. We’ll talk more tonight.” Todd kissed me on the cheek and opened the door so we could leave.

I was in shock. This was not the response I expected. I’m not even sure this was a response I wanted. It was going to be a long day for sure.

Surprisingly, the day flew by, maybe because I didn’t want to have this conversation. I don’t know what I want anymore. I want Todd, I want a baby. I don’t want to be disappointed again. I don’t want to be a disappointment. I want to be pregnant. I don’t want to get my hopes up again. I don't want to see Todd's face when I fail, again. I don't think I want to do another round of IVF. What the hell do I want?

My cell rang as I was getting in the car. It was Todd. "Hi, I'm leaving work now." I said answering the phone.

"Good, let's go to Balducci's, I'm craving their calamari." I could hear the smile in Todd's voice, this is where I would normally make a pregnancy joke. He thought all was right in our world now.

"Sounds good. Are you headed there now?" I asked.

"Just headed home to let the dogs out. Do you want to meet there or at the restaurant?"

"I'll meet you at home, I have to stop by the store, and then I'll be home." I was forever going to the store for tampons, what a wonderful life.

Todd met me in the driveway and opened the passenger door. "Let's take your car." He hopped in and I backed down the driveway again.

Todd tried to make small talk on the way to the restaurant but I was still trying to figure out what I wanted.

After being seated and ordering our appetizers, Todd took my hand. "Jeanie, I love you, please, talk to me."

"I don't know what to say. I thought I had it all figured out, and then you say you are willing to try again." I took a sip of my wine. "The problem is, I don't know if I am."

"Are you talking about our marriage or a baby?" Todd let go of my hand.

"The baby, of course. I thought another round of IVF was what I wanted but I don't know, I don't know if I can go through all of that again. The hormones, the retrieval, the disappointment."

“Then we don’t have to decide. Let’s put this whole baby making business on the back burner and talk about something else.

I sighed, ”Not deciding is deciding. I’m not getting any younger, every day we delay this reduces the chance of pregnancy. Do you really want to be in your 60’s paying for college? We either move forward or we stop completely.”

“What do you want to do Jeanie? I’m fine, either way. I always thought having kids was the most important thing but watching everything you’ve gone through, it just kills me. The most important thing is you, our marriage, the life we have together. Having kids would be a bonus, a wonderful bonus, but our life will still be full and busy and meaningful if we don’t have children.” Todd waited for me to reply.

“I worry that you will resent me. Not today or tomorrow, but one day you’ll look back and think about everything you missed out on by staying married to me. I can’t live with that.” I was doing my best not to cry, thankfully the restaurant was busy and no one was paying attention to us.

"Jeanie, I can't tell you what I will or won't feel in the future, but when I married you, you were enough. Yes, we talked about a family, but that wasn't why I fell in love with you. It was you, just you, all of you, and this is just part of our journey."

I stared at the candle flickering on the table. The light was bouncing off our wine glasses, creating little burst of light.

"I'm not ready to talk about a surrogate, but I don't know if I can go through all of the hormones again. Those things are brutal." I tried to laugh but it was still too fresh and real to be funny.

Todd took a deep breath, "What about the frozen embryos? I've been doing some reading and the pregnancy rate is the same as using fresh embryos and you wouldn't have to take all the medicines you take for a full cycle."

"What if it doesn't work? Those embryos are our safety net, in case we need a surrogate."

"We'll still have a few left. This really would be the last time. Good or bad, we have to move on. If you decide to go through another cycle, fresh or frozen, it has to be with the stipulation that we either start interviewing surrogates, looking at adoption agencies, or decide that enough is enough and we are going to be happy with our life the way it is."

Before I could answer our food came and we dug in. I was starving, I hadn't been eating well; the stress of the last year had caught up with me. I watched Todd when he wasn't looking. I really was so very fortunate to have him. I knew he would be happy, no matter what I decided. And I knew if he did resent me one day, he would never let it show, because ultimately it had been his decision as well.

"Let's do it." I smiled at Todd. "Let's do a frozen cycle. I think I could handle that. I don't want to tell anyone, not even my sisters this time. Let this be just ours. No what if's from everyone else, no questions, no buying out the toy store to make amends to my nieces and nephews. Just us. Our little secret. If it doesn't go well, we'll mourn together. We can take a mini vacation, just the two of us, and then we can decide what to do next. Together, without any outside opinions.

Now, two months later, I'm sitting outside the fertility center, trying to summon up the courage to go get my blood drawn to see if the frozen cycle worked. It feels like the end. I know I will never do this again, and I've come to terms with that. It's now or never. If this didn't work, I will never carry a child. I will never nurse my baby, I will never know what it feels like to know someone before they are born.

As I open the car door my cell phone rings, it's Janie, of course it is. It's always Janie. I silence the phone and head to the building.

Porter's ears

I had been calling both of my sisters all morning and neither one of them was answering. Julie had finally answered her phone. I needed someone to keep the kids so I could run Porter to the pediatrician, he is running a little fever, probably just an ear infection but I don't want to drag everyone to the doctor's office.

Julie said she would get the boys up from their naps and come over. I can't believe her boys still nap. Usually by three my kids are fighting naps and I just let them be done. That's Julie though, no one is messing up her schedule.

The big kids were chasing each other through the house. I took Porter upstairs so I could at least run a brush through my hair before leaving. I grabbed a clean shirt, checked my yoga pants for stains and caught a profile of my swelling belly. Either this baby was going to be huge or he had brought some friends to the party, I was much bigger than with my other kids. My doctor said it was just the result of having my fifth baby so close to the other four, my muscles were tired!

I heard the noise level increase downstairs and knew that Julie and the boys had arrived. Collin loved his cousins, and Lacey and Brie loved anything Collin loved.

“Thanks sister,” I said, coming down the stairs. “This shouldn’t take long, in, out, grab a prescription for his antibiotic, and I’ll be back before you miss me.”

“Sweet boy” Julie said, taking Porter from me. “Aunt Julie is so sorry you don’t feel well.” Julie kissed my baby while I kissed the other three.

“I’ll be back as soon as I can, I know Scott is coming home tonight, you guys must be excited. When will he be done with this traveling?”

"I don't really know. He says things are going well and it shouldn't be much longer, so maybe he'll have some news tonight." Julie picked up Brie who was clinging to her legs, "Go, don't worry about us, we'll be fine until you get back."

"Okay. Love you monkeys, I'll be back as soon as I can." I grabbed my purse and headed to the car.

Porter fell asleep in his car seat on the way to the pediatrician. Poor little guy, he didn't sleep well last night and now I had to wake him from the only nap he'd had all day. I unbuckled the car seat and lifted Porter out, he snuggled right into me, never waking up.

Dr. Pennington was busy, as usual, but the receptionist put us immediately into an exam room when she saw Porter was sleeping. Fifteen minutes later the doctor came in, examined Porter, said it was his ears, wrote the prescription, and we were off.

One benefit of having lots of children is that you really get to know your pediatrician. Dr. Pennington knows I'm not a panicky mom so if I call and say one of the kids is sick, she trusts my instincts.

Porter slept through the entire doctor visit and stopping at the pharmacy, he didn't wake up until we got home.

Julie had the house picked up and the kids doing a craft project. My sister can't stand chaos or mess, so when she is over the kids are always doing organized activities. My kids love it. Although I think they really enjoy our noisy, messy, flying by the seat of your pants style, they also enjoy a little structure when Aunt Julie comes over.

"How is he?" Julie says when we come in.

"Fine, ear infection, just let me get past you to grab the medicine syringe so I can get the first dose of antibiotics in him." I squeezed behind Julie, opened the drawer and the sat Porter on the counter to give him his medicine. I threw the syringe in the sink and Porter stood up and jumped into my arms, excited to be up so high.

"Sister, don't let him jump on you like that, it can't be good for the baby, he's a tank!" Julie smiled when she said it but I could feel the judgement in her words.

Ignoring Julie, I went to each of my kids to marvel over their creations. I was feeling pretty tired and although I appreciated Julie's help, I just wanted her to take her judgement and go. A movie and some couch time was what I had planned for the rest of the afternoon. Bryan was working a little late and said he would grab something for the two of us for dinner so I didn't have to worry about making a big meal.

"Okay boys," Julie said to Sam and Max, "We need to head out, Daddy will be home before we know it."

"Thanks again Julie, I don't know how I would have juggled them all."

"Any time sister," Julie said, heading for the door. "I probably won't see much of you this week, but call if you need anything. Bye guys, love you all so much." Julie kissed each of my kids and then she was gone.

Now to decide which movie will buy me the most quiet time. This momma needs a nap.

Scott has good news

Janie always has the worst timing. Today of all days, she needed a sitter and Scott is coming home. Pulling into the house I gave each of the boys a job to do, I had to get the house inspection ready, and dinner on the table.

I didn't pick Scott up from the airport, he said it was a waste of time and he wanted to come home to a decent meal and not say hello to his boys from the front seat of the car. I knew the real reason, he wanted to catch me off guard.

While the boys were making their beds I started dinner. Meatloaf. I think Scott picked that on purpose, he knew the boys hated it so his first night back home he could set the tone for the next week when I sent the boys to bed hungry. Oh, how I hated him.

Once the meatloaf was in the oven I quickly walked through the house trying to see all the things Scott would notice. There was a rogue sock tucked under the edge of the couch, the damn hamper lid was up again, and the boys' closet door was open. When I was satisfied that Scott would find nothing glaringly wrong, I went back to the kitchen to peel potatoes.

I heard the Uber pull up and called the boys, they came running into the kitchen, excited to see their father. Max's shirt was on inside out, how had I not noticed that? I quickly pulled the shirt over his head

"Daddy!" The boys ran to Scott and he bent down to hug them. When he straightened up he was smiling, "I have some great news." He said walking over to me.

"Are you finished? No more traveling?" I tried to look excited, knowing that's what he expected.

"No, and turn off the oven, we are going out to eat tonight!" Scott carried his bag to the bedroom while the boys ran after him telling him stories from the week.

I stared after him. Scott never wasted food. Scott never changed a plan he made and he certainly never out of the blue wanted to go to a restaurant on a Friday night. What could his news be?

I stood in the kitchen like an idiot. I tried to be excited, the boys certainly were. I could hear them jumping and bouncing and talking over each other. Scott wasn't even correcting their behavior. What kind of fresh hell was in store for me now?

Grabbing the aluminum foil out of the drawer, I pulled the meatloaf out of the oven and turned off the heat under the potatoes. I could save the meatloaf, the potatoes I wasn't sure about. When Scott and the boys came back in the kitchen, I was smiling and ready to go.

"Let's get out of here, we'll go to the pasta place your mother loves." Scott said, herding the boys to the door. "Are you just going to stand there? We have celebrating to do." He was still smiling but the pit in my stomach just kept getting bigger.

Once at the restaurant we got seated almost immediately. I asked Scott what the good news was but he insisted we order first.

The waitress came and took our orders. She was so sweet, even complimenting the boys on ordering for themselves. I hoped she didn't have to witness whatever horrible thing I felt sure was about to happen.

"Can anyone guess what we are celebrating?" Scott asked and I swear, if I didn't know this man I would have said his eyes were twinkling.

"No more traveling!" Max said excitedly.

“That’s not it, Mommy already said that. What about you Sammy, do you have a guess?” Sammy? Scott hadn’t called our son Sammy since his first birthday.

“We get to go with you next time?” The boys had been asking if they could go with their father so for Sam, this would be a dream come true.

“Well, not next time but soon. We’re all moving to Nebraska!” Scott said it like it was the greatest thing in the world.

I swallowed the tea I had been drinking. “What? We can’t move, our home is here.” It was the first thing that came to my mind. Everything I knew and loved was right here, I didn’t want to move.

“We’ll sell it and get a new house. A bigger house, maybe even get a dog.” The waitress came back with our salads and Scott dug in.

“What’s going on?” I asked, my appetite completely gone. “I thought you were almost done there.”

"I am, and it's going so well that the company wants to promote me and have me take over that location. I'm getting promoted to executive vice president. I've been looking at houses, I have some saved on my laptop for you to look at, and I already checked the school district, it's the top in the state." Scott kept eating and joking with the boys like he hadn't just dropped the biggest bomb of our married life.

"I think we should talk about this. Moving, uprooting the boys, our families, it's a lot." I stammered.

Instantly, Scott's mood changed. "Now you are making all the decisions for our family? I'm pretty sure you are not the one paying the mortgage." The look Scott shot me let me know I would pay for that particular outburst.

Just then our cute waitress came back with our food. I looked at the table, anywhere to keep from making eye contact with Scott, I could feel him glaring at me. In my purse my phone started ringing.

"Is that your phone?" Scott said, knowing that it was.

"Sorry, in the rush to get here I forgot to turn it off." I reached into my purse, it was Janie. I silenced it and turned the ringer off. Before I could put the phone in my purse, it started vibrating, Janie again. Ignoring it, I put the phone away.

"No phones at dinner Mommy." Sam said. Apparently my boys know the rules for my behavior too.

"Sorry bud, I just forgot to turn it off, it won't happen again." I went back to picking at my dinner while Scott and the boys made plans for our new life. I could feel my phone vibrate every few minutes. Janie probably thought we would love to come over and spend time with her and Bryan tonight. My sister, always oblivious to what's going on with everyone else.

What's wrong with Janie?

Opening the door between the kitchen and garage my babies, Sophie and Jack were waiting to greet me. It's true what they say about childless couples doting on the pets. We certainly catered to these two, but I couldn't imagine that changing even if we had a child. I scooped each of my fur kids up in turn and give them a kiss and a cuddle. "I'm home honey, did you eat already? I can throw something together if you haven't" I walked into the dining room and felt tears spring to my eyes.

The room was lit by candlelight, the table was set with our best dishes and next to those, Chinese take-out boxes, my favorite comfort food.

Todd came around the table and wrapped me in his arms, "I love you Jeanie, whatever is meant to be, will be and whatever happens tomorrow will not change what we have." I had asked Dr. Garcia to give me 24 hours before calling with the test results, I just wanted one last night of hope.

I leaned into my husband, the man who I wasn't sure I deserved. When we first married we talked about "someday." The house we would have, the jobs, the cars, the vacations, and the children. We agreed early on we wanted three and never thought for a second those babies wouldn't come. We worked hard, saved money, bought a house, saved some more money and decided we were ready to have a baby. What we didn't know was that all that money we saved, all those dreams we had, everything would be spent chasing the one thing we could not have- a child.

"Sweetie, I don't know what I did to deserve you, you have been so wonderful through all of this."

"We are in this together, good or bad, it's ours, together. How are you feeling? Anything new or different?"

“No, same as always at this stage, crampy, my boobs hurt, I'm tired, cranky. I wouldn't be surprised if I didn't get my period before they call in the morning.”

“Baby I'm sorry,” Todd was pulling my chair out, “I don't know what to say to make this right. I guess we just have to look forward, to our opportunity to try something else.”

“Yes it is, let's try to look at this as a celebration. I've gone through enough hormone injections that I don't actually need to get pregnant to experience the mood swings! So this is a new beginning, a chance to try again. Do we still have a bottle of wine downstairs?”

“We still have several bottles of wine downstairs but do you think that's a good idea, I mean, what if.....?” Todd didn't finish the sentence but I could see the hope in his eyes and I didn't want to rain on his hopes.

"Even if, one glass of wine won't hurt anything, I've actually heard that an occasional glass of wine while you're pregnant is thought to be healthy. Everything in moderation."

Todd went downstairs and returned with a bottle of wine, the opener, and two glasses. He went into the kitchen, rinsed the glasses, and poured the wine. When he brought our wine glasses in I was filling our plates. "This is so wonderful, you always know exactly what I need."

As we raised our glasses to toast our uncertain future, my cell phone rang. It was Janie, I hit ignore so we could get back to dinner. Before I even got my fork to my mouth the house phone rang. Todd went into the kitchen to check the caller id.

"It's Janie, it must be important, it's not like her to call the house phone."

"I'll call her after we eat. She's been calling all day and I just wasn't up to dealing with her. Is that your cell phone? What the hell?" Todd grabbed his phone and hit the call button. Immediately, his face changed. “Okay, buddy, we are on our way. Did you call your Daddy?” He covered the phone and said to me, “Get your shoes, something is wrong with Janie.”

We were in the car before Todd hung up the phone. “That was Collin, Janie was on the other line crying, Collin said there is blood, lots of blood. What the hell?”

“Did she fall? Did she cut herself?” She sounded fine in the ten messages she left earlier, it couldn't be anything too serious.

“Collin didn't say, he said he called Daddy but he didn't answer, he called Julie but she didn't answer then he called you and you didn't answer so he called me.” I could tell Todd was frightened, he drove like a mad man. I didn't know what to say, I couldn't wrap my mind around something being wrong with my sister. This was the woman who gave birth to her babies, came home immediately and made pancakes for the other kids to celebrate having a new sibling. Nothing stopped her or slowed her down.

When we pulled up there was an ambulance parked halfway on the sidewalk and Julie's car was turning in behind us. 'What's wrong?" Julie asked, jumping out of the car and heading up the sidewalk.

"I don't know, Collin told Todd there was blood and Janie was crying."

"We were eating dinner, the message on my phone was just Collin crying and telling the girls Mommy was going to be ok. I've been calling the whole way over here but no one answers."

The front door opened and the paramedics were wheeling my sister out on a stretcher, moving very quickly.

"I can't, please, my babies, there's no one here with my babies." Janie was crying, then she saw us. "Thank God, stay with my babies, tell them I'm okay, tell them I'll be back soon."

My heart dropped, Janie was covered with blood and more blood was soaking through the sheet that was covering her. "What's wrong with my sister? Someone tell me what's going on!"

Bryan came running up, trying to grab Janie's hands, trying to find out what's going on. "Can someone stay with the kids?" Bryan was climbing in the ambulance with Janie, the kids were crying, trying to get to their parents.

"Don't worry, we've got the kids. Tell Janie we'll be there shortly." Julie said, herding the kids in the house. "Come here babies, it's okay." Julie looked at me, "Jeanie will you go get Porter, I can hear him crying." I hurried to the stairs while Julie comforted the kids.

"Hey, big guy, come to Aunt Jeanie, it's okay, don't cry Munchkin. Let's get you in a clean diaper then we'll go downstairs, how does that sound?" Porter was smiling before I even got him out of the crib. Janie's babies were all criers but always settled down quickly.

I got Porter changed and headed back downstairs. Julie was sitting on the couch, three little tear stained faces hanging on to her every word. "Sometimes Mommies get sick, just like everyone else. Right now, your Mommy is sick so those men in the ambulance are taking her to the doctor so he can find out why she is sick and try to make her feel better."

"Is she gonna get a shot? Sometimes when I go to the doctor when I'm not sick I have to get a shot. I don't think Mommy will like it if they give her a shot." Collin was worried about his Mommy getting a shot, little things seem so big and scary when you're small.

"Mommy may have to get a shot, but your Daddy is there so if she has to get a shot, he will hold her hand and that will make it okay. Then she can come home and you guys can all give her kisses until she feels better."

"Us too, Mommy? We want Aunt Janie to feel better." Sam and Max looked almost as frightened as Janie's kids.

"Yes, you too, my big boys. Now, Aunt Jeanie and I need to go to the doctor with your Mommy and Daddy, but you guys get to stay with Uncle Scott and Uncle Todd." Julie turned to Todd, "I don't think Janie fed the kids yet, they usually eat late because Bryan gets home late. Maybe you can round up something for dinner?" Then she looked at Scott, "At least Porter is off the breast that will make this easier. Try to get the kids to bed early, they need some down time."

"We need a bath, Mommy said." That was Lacey, that girl would live in the bath if you let her. Julie looked at Scott, "Looks like baths before bed. Use the tub in Janie's bathroom for the girls and the tub in the hall bath for the boys that way you can get them all bathed at the same time. I'll run upstairs and grab pajamas for everyone and put them on the Collin's bed."

"You guys go, we have this, we can handle the kids, you two go to your sister." I could tell that Todd was frightened by all the blood he saw, just as we were.

I kissed Todd while Julie kissed all the kids, jumped in the car and headed to the hospital. "What do you think is wrong?" I asked Julie, "What would cause all that blood?"

"I have no idea, I saw her today, she was fine, just tired."

"Well, pregnancy makes you tired, or so I've heard." I tried to smile, make the moment more lighthearted, but I was terrified.

"I just can't figure out where the blood came from." Julie was more thinking out loud than actually talking to me. "You don't bleed that much when you are in labor, and it's much too early for labor. Janie always has the easiest labors too."

I let Julie think out loud and stared out the window, what would make anyone bleed like that? Julie parked by the emergency entrance and we ran inside and up to the admitting desk.

“Hi, our sister was just brought in by ambulance, Jane Starrett, which room is she in?” Julie, ever efficient wanted to get back there with Janie.

“Let's see, Mrs. Starrett has been taken to delivery, it’s on the third floor, if you take this elevator..”

“Delivery? For what? She's not due, she can't deliver now.” I was feeling a little frantic.

“As I said, take this elevator up to the third floor, make a right, follow that hall to the end, make another right and the nurses desk will be on the left.”

Julie and I were in the elevator almost before the nurse stopped speaking. Delivery? What the hell is going on, Janie was only about six months pregnant, how could she be delivering?

As soon as the elevator opened, Julie and I ran down the hall. It felt almost like when you run in a dream and can't get anywhere. The nurses spotted us coming around the corner, they knew instinctively who we were there to see.

"Janie, Jane Starrett, where is she?" Julie was out of breath, more from fear I think than from running.

"Let's go down the hall, there's a waiting room and I'll let Mr. Starrett know you're here." The nurse was trying to guide us down the hall.

"I'm not going anywhere, I want to see my sister, what room is she in? Why do you people have her in a delivery room anyway? Are you crazy? She is only six months pregnant! What room, or do I have to start checking them all?"

"I'm sorry, you are going to have to wait in the waiting room. Your sister is having complications and the last thing the doctor needs is two additional people in that room. Would you like some coffee, ice water? I promise I'll tell your brother in law as soon as he comes out." As she said that the pagers the nurses were carrying went off and the nurse we were talking to and the other one still behind the desk rushed down the hall and into a room.

Julie and I ran behind them, we tried to enter the room as they were pushing Bryan out. Bryan was crying and calling Janie's name, the nurses shut the door in his face. I grabbed Bryan and hugged him, I felt Julie's arms go around both of us. "What's wrong, what's wrong with Janie? No one will tell us anything. Is she okay? Where did all that blood come from? Why do they have her in delivery?" Julie and I were talking over each other asking the same questions over and over while Bryan cried.

"The baby, the doctor said it doesn't look good, they are trying.... Janie is bleeding too much... they are trying to stop the bleeding....trying to save.... I've never seen so much blood...."

"What is going on? Why is Janie bleeding?" Julie was trying to get Bryan to make sense, he was crying so hard, most of the time all we could understand was Janie and blood, he kept saying over and over, there's so much blood.

“I don't know” Bryan slid down the wall, sobbing. Julie and I looked at each other. This cannot be happening.

We tried to get Bryan to tell us what was going on but the more we tried, the harder he cried. The only thing we could understand was that they were trying to save Janie. What? What does that mean? Why do they need to save Janie? She is healthy, she's only pregnant, not having a heart attack. Julie marched up to the nurse’s desk and demanded to know what was going on. The nurses weren't much help, apparently Janie was in trouble and people were running in and out of her room. They wheeled her past us, running, we tried to keep up but when they got the doors of the operating room they gently pushed us and told us we would have to wait. No one would tell us anything.

Julie and I found a waiting room and got Bryan into a chair. Julie ran to get him a drink while I tried to calm him down. I didn't know what to say because I had no idea what was going on, I was completely out of my realm.

When Julie came back she tried to talk to Bryan. He just sobbed, and he kept begging us to tell the doctors not to let Janie die.

What in the hell is going on? Do people die from pregnancy? Here I was, dying to be pregnant, I never realized you could die from being pregnant. Julie and I walked the floor for what seemed like hours. We called and checked on the kids, so at least we were able to tell Bryan they were okay.

Finally, Dr. Merrill, Janie's obstetrician came in, he looked exhausted.

"Janie is stable. She had us worried for a while there. That's the good news, the bad news is," he hesitated and looked at Bryan, "We had to give her a hysterectomy to stop the bleeding."

Bryan just sat, looking stunned, I'm not even sure he understood what the doctor said. Julie jumped right in.

“Why? Why did you have to give her a hysterectomy? Why was she bleeding like that?”

“Janie had a placenta abruption. What that means is that the placenta tore away from the uterine wall prior to labor and delivery. Most abruptions are small, partial tears. They present some danger to mother and fetus, but usually with bedrest and close supervision we are able to take the pregnancy to the point that the fetus is viable.”

“And Janie's baby? Is it going to be ok?”

“No, I'm sorry, the fetus didn't make it. We believe she passed away before Janie even called for help.”

“Stop calling my baby a fetus. It was a girl, she was a girl?” These were the first intelligible words Bryan had uttered since we got to the hospital.

“I'm sorry Bryan, you're right, the baby. Yes, she was a girl, a beautiful, perfectly formed, little girl. I'm so sorry.” Bryan was sobbing again.

“How am I going to tell Janie? She lives for her kids.”

“I'm sorry Bryan, unfortunately blood loss with a placenta abruption is a common problem, as is the body’s inability to clot after an abruption, and that's what happened to Janie. We tried to have her deliver vaginally, that is what we were doing earlier, but when Janie's vitals had dropped to an alarming level we knew our best chance to stop the bleeding was to perform a cesarean. Once we got the f.. the baby out we tried to stop the bleeding, to get Janie's body to heal itself, and when it didn't the risk of losing Janie was too high. We had to take the uterus out.”

The room was absolutely quiet except for Bryan's sobs. Even Julie, ever present, ever questioning, take charge Julie, had nothing to say.

"Janie will be in recovery for about an hour and then we will take her to her room, and Bryan you can see her then. She has the baby with her. As soon as she was stable the nurses placed the baby on her chest."

Dr. Merrill left the room. Julie and I looked at each other, that unspoken sister code, we needed to get out of this room.

"Bryan, Jeanie and I are going to run to the restroom, will you be ok for a few minutes?"

Bryan just waved us off, never taking his head out of his hands. Julie and I quickly left the room and walked down the hall.

"How could this happen? Why didn't they know? Why didn't they do something about it?" I could not understand how this could happen. My sister was a pro at this pregnancy thing.

“I don't know. I don't know.” Julie's eyes were darting up and down the hall like she was waiting for someone to come and tell us this was all a mistake.

I started crying, I couldn't help it. “Do you think Janie is going to be okay? She has to be okay. Losing the baby is enough, we can't lose Janie too.” I'm sobbing almost as hard as Bryan. As much as my sisters make me crazy, a world without either of them is not something I want to imagine.

Julie put her arms around me, I could feel her tears wetting my cheeks, right along with mine. “Janie is going to be just fine. She is our baby sister, no way I'm letting her cut out before me. That's one of the many perks of being the oldest, I don't have to bury my sisters, I get to go first. So yes, Janie will be fine.” She took my face in her hands trying to hold back her sobs, “It’s not her turn dammit!” With that Julie broke down. That scared me almost more than what the doctor had to say. Julie doesn't cry, she takes care of everyone and everything. If she cries, she does it when she's alone. I've never seen it.

Finally, Julie pulled away from me, trying to swallow her tears, "Let's go the restroom and wash our faces. The last thing Bryan needs is to see that we are upset too. Are you going to be able to keep it together when we go in there?'

I nodded, I didn't yet trust myself to speak. We walked to the restroom and washed our faces in silence, both lost in our own thoughts. I don't know what Julie was thinking, but I was pissed at my mother. Where was she when Janie needed her most? After my father's death, my mother never seemed to recover. She took very little interest in her daughters and she passed away right after before I graduated. Everyone said she died of a broken heart, but her daughter's knew the truth, vodka was her constant companion after Daddy's death and it was the alcohol that killed her. Sometimes I hated her for that.

When we got back to the little waiting room Bryan was trying to pull himself together. He said the nurse had been in and he would be able to see Janie in about fifteen minutes. Now it was his turn to go to the restroom and wash his face.

Shortly after Bryan returned a nurse came to get him. Julie and I asked if we could go as well and were told that because Janie was still pretty out of it, we had to wait. The nurse also told us that the hospital had a photographer on the way to take pictures of the baby so Janie and Bryan would always have them.

We sat to wait, again.

How does this happen?

I am not equipped to deal with this. That's the first thing I want to tell everyone. This is too much. Janie, Jeanie and I have buried both of our parents and our grandparents that was hard enough. This I had no point of reference for, no skills to fall back on, no one to hold my hand and help me soothe my sister.

Sometimes it sucks being the oldest. I always feel responsible for everyone. After our father died, our mother basically forgot that we were real human beings who might occasionally need a little interaction from their mother. Oh, she made sure we had all the things we needed, we were fed, and clothed, and always had a roof over our heads, but the one thing we needed most, a parent, she was unable to give us.

Now, Janie's baby has died, Janie has almost died, and I don't know how to help her. I don't know what to say. All I really want to do is go home and hug my boys until they push me away and say “too tight, Momma,” before they go running off to their next adventure. I want my babies. I also want my sister's babies. I want to gather all those warm little ones to me and tell them that everything is going to be okay. Momma will come home and she will be just fine. Would I be lying to them? Is Janie going to be 'just fine'?

I look over at Jeanie. Shit, she is falling apart. I can't do this. I see in her face that she is scared. She has tried so long to get pregnant and now she is afraid.

“Neen” I can only call her that when it is just us, otherwise she gets pissed, “It’s going to be okay. The doctor said Janie was stable.” I don't want to bring up the fear I know she has for herself.

“How does this happen? Pregnancy is supposed to be such a happy time. For a minute I was scared for myself, but then I realized with my track record that's not likely, but now, how can I ask someone else to take this risk for me?” Jeanie said through her tears.

“Sweetie, you know this is not the norm. Women have babies every day, this is a fluke. Just because it happened to Janie doesn't mean it will happen to your surrogate. You have to stop thinking like that. After everything you've gone through it's your time to have this turn out right for once. Look at us, between Janie and I, we have had five completely trouble free pregnancies.”

Jeanie looked at up at me, “I wanted one of you to be my surrogate. Now I feel so selfish, I was willing to risk one of my sisters for a baby. I didn't know this could happen”

“First of all Jeanie, no one knew this could happen. I'm touched that you would have wanted me to carry your baby. I don't even know what to say about that, but I do believe this will not happen again.”

“Do you know how many times I was jealous of Janie? How many times I wondered, why her? Why crazy, unorganized Janie? Why couldn't I have just one baby, instead of her having baby after baby after baby? It never seemed fair, I thought she had more than her share and that she had no business having another baby. Now look what happened." Jeanie was really sobbing now.

"This is not your fault, you did not wish this on your sister."

"But I did, that's what you don't understand. I wished that just once you two would understand what it was like to be me and not get what you wanted when you wanted it."

"Jeanie, that's silly, first of all, you cannot wish a health problem on someone, those things are completely beyond our control. Second, I understand. There were times when I thought Janie was nuts and that she should stop having babies. I mean seriously, her house is like a zoo, why does she keep having more? But that doesn't mean that we caused this. As much as we both thought Janie should stop having babies, neither one of us would wish this on anyone, let alone our sister. Now stop this. Bryan will be coming back and we have to help him help Janie and the kids and we can't do that if we are feeling sorry for ourselves."

Jeanie and I sat on the waiting room couch, our heads together, comforting each other, until Bryan came back in. He told us we could go see Janie now. They had taken the baby awa,y but that was okay. All I really wanted was to see my sister, hold her hand, and know that she was alright.

My worst nightmare

When I woke up it was dark. The room was dark and filled with the nighttime noises of a hospital, but still I could hear Bryan breathing. That sound, more than anything else, comforted me. Bryan is my rock. He gets me. When everyone else thinks I'm crazy, Bryan understands.

I'm not sure why I'm here, but I'm the one in the bed, so at least I know it's me and not Bryan, one of the kids, or my sisters. I try to sit up, but my chest and stomach feel like there is a huge weight sitting on them. What in the hell happened? Was I in a car accident? Are the kids okay? I want to get out of bed when it hits me. I remember.

I remember the pain, and the blood, so much blood. I remember talking to my baby, asking him or her to be okay, just hang in there, Momma is gonna make this better. I put my hand on my belly, it doesn't have the firmness it had this morning, it has more of the squishy, after baby feel. What has happened to my baby? I know it is too early, nowhere near time for me to have had the baby. What's wrong?

"Bryan." I say his name so softly I'm sure he won't hear me, but he does, he always does.

"Hey baby, you're awake. How are you feeling?" Bryan kisses my forehead and strokes my hair, the same thing he has done a million times in our married life when we wake up together.

"What happened? Where is the baby? I want our baby, make them bring me our baby. What did they do to me? I hurt, everything hurts. Bryan, I want my baby." I'm crying and I don't know why, I just know that something is not right, something has gone very, very wrong. I hear other people moving in the room. My sisters are here, that's when I know, this is a very bad thing. Always in my life, my sisters have been there for me, all the good times, they have celebrated with me. This time however, they are very, very quiet, not celebrating at all.

“Hey baby sister, how are you feeling?” Julie asked, I feel Jeanie take my hand, rubbing her finger in my palm like she's done since I was a little girl.

“I don't know how I'm feeling because I don't know what's wrong. My stomach and chest are sore and my belly feels like jello. Where's my baby? What have they done with my baby? Julie, go talk to someone, make them fix this.” I can't stop crying.

I can hear Bryan and Julie and Jeanie whispering, but I don't know what they are saying. The door to my room opens and someone goes out. Julie comes back in and tells Bryan the doctor will be in shortly.

“I don't want them to come in and knock me out again, I want to know what is going on, I want my baby!” I tried to get up, Bryan bear hugged me so I couldn't keep trying. Not that I could, everything hurt. I must have cried myself to sleep because the next thing I knew the overhead light was on and my doctor was standing beside me, holding my hand.

“Hey Janie, how are you feeling?”

“I don't know Dr. Merrill, why don’t you tell me? What in the hell is going on? I feel like I'm in the twilight zone. I don't know how I feel, everything hurts and I don't know why and no one will tell me.” I was trying not to sob but not having much luck.

“Tell me what you remember, let's start there.” Dr. Merrill said while checking my chart.

“I remember, after I took Porter to the pediatrician, I was so tired. I put on a movie for the kids and laid on the couch. Porter woke me up and I got up to fix the kids something to eat. I was holding Porter and my stomach started hurting really badly. I went into our bedroom, I thought maybe I had to go to the bathroom but I suddenly felt weak and sat down on the bed. I thought my water broke, but when I looked down it was blood. After that I only remember pieces. I remember my sisters at the house, then I remember being on a stretcher and.... I don't know. What's wrong with me? Is the baby okay?”

“First of all, you are going to be fine. You had us a little worried but you are going to be fine. As for the baby...” Dr. Merrill stopped and looked at Bryan. I saw him shake his head slightly. “Janie, we lost the baby.”

The room started to go gray, if I had been standing I would have fallen, my ears were ringing and I heard this horrible keening. My sisters and my husband rushed to the bed, trying to get me to calm down, that keening was coming from be but even once I realized it I couldn't make it stop.

“What happened? What did I do? What can I do? I want my baby...” My sobs tore out of me like a thing alive. How could this happen? Dr. Merrill waited patiently, holding my hand. I heard him say to Bryan, “Maybe we should have the nurse bring her something.”

“No, she has to know, the longer we go without telling her the truth the harder it will be.” Bryan was crying as well.

"Have you no heart Bryan? She needs time to rest, time to adjust, we don't have to rehash this." That was Julie, always trying to protect me from everything.

"I want to know, I want to know right now. What happened to my baby?" I'm trying to control my crying, knowing that if I don't, they may never tell me.

Dr. Merrill said, "I'm so sorry Janie, I know how much you wanted this baby. You had a complication called placenta abruption. During placenta abruption, the placenta pulls away from the uterine wall before delivery. Yours was severe, you had a complete abruption, the fetus had passed away before you even go to the hospital." He waited while I moaned and thrashed, my baby, my beautiful little baby, what had I done?

"Did I do this? What did I do that caused this? Did I pick up Porter too much? What was it?

"You have none of the risk factors associated with this condition. This will happen sometimes if there is a trauma to the abdomen, high blood pressure in the mother, carrying multiples, you had none of those things. The only thing that would slightly increase your risk of an abruption is that this was your fifth pregnancy."

"So having too many babies caused my baby to die?" I'm almost hiccupping with the effort of trying to stop my sobs. My poor little baby. "Where is my baby? I want my baby. What was it? We didn't even find out..." I can't stop the tears.

"She was beautiful, honey," Bryan said stroking my hair, "She looked like Lacey when she was born, but so much smaller." I could see Bryan struggling to hold back his tears.

"I want her, I want my baby, right now, someone bring her to me." I tried to get out of the bed, my abdomen felt like it was on fire. "What's wrong with me? And why don't I remember her being born?"

"Janie, you have to stay in bed. We tried to deliver the baby vaginally, we knew she had already passed away so there was no danger to her, but your bleeding would not stop. We had to do an emergency cesarean....... and we had to give you a hysterectomy to stop the bleeding." I could see the pain in Dr. Merrill's eyes. He and a midwife had taken care of me through all of my pregnancies, and he came to see me immediately after I delivered each time.

At first, all I could think about was the baby, I wanted her, I wanted to hold her and tell her how much I loved her, how I had loved her since the day my period was late. "Please, I need to see her. Please, please, Bryan, make them bring our baby to me." I was trying to curl up in a ball and just cry, but I couldn't, my stomach was hurting and empty. I suddenly realized it would forever be empty.

"Did you say hysterectomy? Did you give me a hysterectomy without my consent?" Suddenly I was furious. Not only did this man let my baby die but he took away any chance of me ever having another baby. I pushed Dr. Merrill off my bed. "Get away from me! You never asked me what I wanted. You just did what was easiest. First you let my baby die, then you play God and decide I don't get to have any more children? Get out of here!" If I could have gotten out of bed I think I would have hit him, over and over and over again.

Dr. Merrill stood by the bed, "I understand how you feel. There wasn't time to ask you, there wasn't time to ask Bryan, you were bleeding out. We tried everything but it came down to the hysterectomy or letting you die. I'm sorry, there simply wasn't another option. I will tell the nurse to bring your daughter to you." Then he turned and walked out of the room.

"Oh, sweetie, I'm so, so sorry. I.." Jeanie was trying to comfort me, but I cut her off mid-sentence.

"Don't tell me you know how I feel. You don't, you have no idea. You either Julie, with your perfect little children and your perfect life, nothing bad ever happens to you. Get out, both of you get out of my room. Leave! Now!" I was screaming but couldn't help myself. Bryan was holding me and letting me rock back and forth against him. I saw that my sisters were hurt, but I didn't care. Why should I be the only one to ever hurt?

The midwife who had delivered all of my babies came into my room. “Hi Janie, Dr. Merrill is having the baby brought to you, and I just want to talk to you a little bit before she gets here. Now first of all, she is going to look like your other babies, but she is much, much smaller. She is also going to be a little stiff. I do want you to know that she did not feel any pain, our best estimate is that within minutes of your abruption she passed away, probably before you even realized you were in serious trouble.” Sarah took my hand, “Look at me, Janie, I want to tell you the story of your daughter's birth. I know how important your kids birth stories are, and how you tried to have everything just so, and since you were not awake when she was born, I want to tell you her birth story.” She looked from me to Bryan and asked, “Had you picked a name yet?”

My sobs were now just hiccups, I looked at Bryan, “We didn't know she was a girl, we talked about names but hadn't really decided, we were pretty convinced she was a boy.”

"It doesn't matter, we called her little love in the delivery room. Dr. Merrill was trying to let you deliver vaginally, do you remember that?" I shook my head. "Probably because your blood loss was so great, when he saw that we were not able to stop your bleeding and it looked like we might lose you as well, he decided to do the c-section. When he made the incision and reach in to grab her, he put his hand under her little bum to lift her out and one of her little feet popped out. The tiniest, most perfect little foot you ever saw. One of the nurses had heated up blankets, even though we knew she was gone, we wanted her to be wrapped in warmth. When Dr. Merrill handed her to the nurse she said, she is so delicate, like a little flower. As she wrapped the baby in those blankets she said, 'welcome to the world little love, we are all so sad you couldn't stay', then she handed her to me. I held your daughter and talked to her while Dr. Merrill took care of you. As soon as he was finished, and you were relatively stable we put little love on your chest and covered the two of you with a blanket. The first time Bryan saw her she was wrapped up with you. That is your baby's birth story. She was handled gently, everyone spoke softly to her, as if she could hear us. We kept her warm and talked to her until we could put her in your arms." As she finished speaking a nurse walked in the room with a very tiny bundle in her arms, my sisters trailing behind her.

I was more afraid than I had ever been in my life. I don't know how to explain it other than to say that the nurse was about to lay my worst fear in my arms. I wanted so badly to hold her, I ached for her, but at the same time, I didn't want to see her little face, knowing she would never wake up.

I think every mother, probably every parent, has those heart stopping moments. The moments you think something has happened to your child. I remember the first time Collin slept through the night, I was terrified when I woke up, looked at the clock and realized that my three month old had not called for me during the night. I remember my heart pounding, my head growing fuzzy, my palms were sweating, and suddenly I was shivering.

Being the huge coward I am, I rolled over to Bryan, snuggled up against him and said, “I hear Collin will you go get him for me?” Yes, I'm a wimp, I was not going into that room if something was wrong with my baby. When Bryan came in my relief was so huge I started crying. I let him assume it was hormonal, I couldn't bring myself to tell him why I was crying. That was the last night Collin slept in his own room.

I felt that way now. Except I knew something was wrong and there was absolutely nothing I could do. “Bryan, would you like to hold her?” I just didn't have the courage.

“No, sweetie, I'll hold her when you are done.”

“I can't imagine that I will ever be done, you guys need to hold her first because I want to be the last person to hold her, and I'm afraid I won't be able to let her go once I get her. Jeanie? Julie?”

My sisters looked at each other. I knew they didn't want to do this either, they didn't want to have to say hello and goodbye in the same breath.

Finally, Jeanie spoke up, her voice shaking, “Let Aunt Jeanie see you, little one. We've waited so long for you.” My heart shattered, those were the exact same words Jeanie said upon seeing each of her nieces and nephews for the first time.

I watched the nurse hand this little blanketed person to my sister. I watched my sister as she said, "Oh, you were worth the wait, what a beauty you are." Then Jeanie, our family storyteller and history keeper, told my baby girl her story. This was one of the things my kids loved most, from the day they were born Jeanie loved telling them the story of how they came into our family, and she did the same with the newest little one.

I had to look away, I was grateful Jeanie was quietly talking to the baby, it made it easier to tune her out. The other stories she told had changed and grown as the kids had grown, but this story would never change. I still could not wrap my brain around that.

I finally heard Jeanie say, "We all love you so much, but you have much more important work to do than entertain us. We will never forget you and when we see you again, you can tell us the rest of your story." Then she kissed my baby girl and handed her to Julie. Jeanie had to leave the room, I knew my sisters were trying so hard to be strong for me.

Julie was cradling the baby, running her finger down her tiny cheek, over and over again, then she started to sing. Her sweet, beautiful voice, singing the hymns we had learned from our grandmother. Bryan was holding my hand and I was trying desperately not to keep squeezing his. I wanted Julie to stop, stop singing my baby to Jesus. When I was a little girl, one of my grandmother's friends had passed away. I asked why she had to go to the funeral and Gram said when someone died you had a funeral to sing them to Jesus to make sure he recognized them as one of his own. At the same time, it was comforting. There is comfort in rituals, even ones we don't like.

I shut my eyes and lay back in the bed, just listening to Julie sing. I must have dozed off because Bryan was waking me up, telling me my daughter was waiting. I scootched myself up on the bed. I lifted my arms to take her from him and I saw her little face. I know they said I saw her in recovery but I have no memory of that but I will never forget that first glimpse of her little plump cheek and button nose when her Daddy was handing her to me.

I was taking deep, slow breaths, trying not to cry. I wanted to remember everything about her, I didn't want my tears to blur my vision. She weighed nothing, little tiny bit of fluff. The nurses had dressed her. She had a bow in her hair, or what would have been hair, given time. That little yellow bow made me think of when my others girls were born. I pushed those thoughts away, I wanted only her, I wanted to fill my memory with every detail.

As I stared into her little face, trying to memorize every detail I looked at Bryan, “Her name is Lily.” My beautiful Lily was swaddled in a blanket, I laid her on the bed and unfolded the blanket from around her. Someone had found a tiny little yellow sleeper that said Angel on the front of it. Her little fingers were curled, her palm barely as wide as my pinky. Her skin was almost translucent. She was beautiful. I just stared. There was so much I wanted to say to her, so much to tell her, that we love her and we wanted her, and a million other things but I couldn't bring myself to break the silence.

After a little bit, I had Bryan help me lay back down, sitting up was torture with the incision and I wanted to lay down and put her on my chest. I cried again, just holding Lily against me, in the spot she would have spent so much time if only she could have stayed.

A nurse came in the room and said she needed to take Lily now. “Can’t we have a little longer, we've only had her with us for a few minutes.” I wasn't ready, please no, I'm not ready.

“I know, the time passes so quickly. The doctors will be doing their rounds shortly, and Dr. Merrill wants to be able to examine you.” When she said that I noticed for the first time that the room was filled with daylight, not artificial hospital light. Bryan was in the hospital bed next to me and my sisters were sleeping in chairs, leaning on each other.

“What time is it? I didn't realize...” I didn't finish the sentence because I wasn't sure what I didn't realize. “Bryan, where are the kids?”

“The kids are fine honey, Todd and Scott stayed with them so they are probably organizing the pantry as we speak.”

My sisters started stirring and realized it was time to say our final goodbyes. Jeanie came to the side of the bed and leaned down to give Lily a kiss. “Can I take some pictures of her with my phone before we have to let her go?'

“Of course.” I said, looking at the nurse.

“Let me open the curtains so the light is better.” She walked to the window and let the sun in, “I'll be back in a few minutes.”

After the nurse left we all got our phones out and took as many pictures as they could hold. Then the nurse came and took Lily away. I really don't remember much after that except that I cried so much I could barely open my eyes.

What happens now?

What do you say when a child dies? Any child? I never know what to say when anyone dies, but my niece? My baby sister's baby? There are no words, so I did the only thing I could do. I went to Janie's and took care of the kids. By the time we left the hospital it was almost dinner time. I had called Scott and told him that Jeanie and I would stop and get pizza for dinner. In the hospital we had decided we wouldn't tell the kids anything, just that Janie had to stay another day but she was fine and would be home tomorrow.

Dr. Merrill said Janie was doing well, but they wanted to keep her one more night for observation then she could come home in the morning

We pulled up in front of Janie's house, we needed to relieve our husbands. Jeanie had taken a leave for the week but our hubbies had to get back to the real world. I opened the door to the kitchen and the kids came running. My boys were so happy to see me, just looking at them was almost more than I could bear. What if I had lost one of them and never got to know them? I put the pizza on the counter and Jeanie and I got down in the floor so this squirming mass of children could say hello. The hugs were almost too much. Janie's children were clinging to us, asking for their Mommy and Daddy. Poor little Porter, he just looked confused.

Jeanie and I go the kids around the table and doled out pizza and drinks. Janie's house looked like a bomb went off in it. Usually it was controlled chaos here anyway but with the men in charge the control had been lost, now it was just chaos. Cleaning would be first on my list, I couldn't let Janie come home to this mess.

Scott tapped me on the shoulder, "How is Janie?"

"Janie is doing well, we'll talk about everything after the kids go down tonight, I don't want to take the chance that they might overhear." I kissed my husband's cheek, knowing he expected it.

“Is Momma coming home?” Collin asked, his mouth full of pizza.

“Don't talk with your mouth full sweetie, you'll choke. No, Momma is not coming home tonight, she is feeling much better but the doctor wants her to stay at the hospital one more night just to make sure she is feeling perfect before she comes home.”

Collin's little face fell. “Mommy never spends the night away, she always comes home.”

“I know bud, but this is kind of a special occasion. Mom really needs to do what the doctor tells her. You know she would run home to you if she could.”

That seemed to cheer him up and he went back to his pizza and talking about the game they were playing before we got there.

The evening raced by. The guys had not bathed the children and they all looked like they were homeless. Even Brie, the girly girl, was only in a diaper and shirt. After dinner, Jeanie and I did a bath assembly line, even with the two of us it still took almost two hours to get all six kids bathed and ready for bed. How does Janie do this every day?

Porter went to sleep first. Poor little guy, he seemed exhausted and fell asleep in Jeanie's arms almost before I was finished buttoning his pajamas. The other kids wanted stories, and not just any story. Aunt Jeanie was there so they wanted a cousin story.

We threw all the bedding on the floor of Collin's room and settled all five big kids in there and Jeanie sat down to tell them a cousin story. One by one, the kids started yawning and rubbing their eyes. It only took about fifteen minutes for all five to fall asleep. Jeanie and I tiptoed out and went back downstairs to our husbands.

"What a day. I can't believe it's only been twenty four hours. It seems much, much longer."

"I know." Jeanie said, " I feel so bad I didn't answer Janie's calls yesterday, but she sounded fine on the voicemails."

“She was fine,” I said, cleaning up the kids plates, “I was here yesterday while she took Porter in for his ear infect… oh man, I totally forgot he needed his antibiotic. Guess we’ll start that again in the morning.”

“What happened?” Todd asked. “How do you go from just fine to a hysterectomy and a lost baby?” The guys were as confused about all of this as we were, probably more so because at least we heard the doctors explanation. It still didn't make it easy to comprehend.

Jeanie and I explained to our husbands what had happened in the past twenty four hours. Telling them about the baby, saying goodbye to her, was so hard. We showed them the pictures we had taken with our phones.

“What happens now?” Todd asked. “Do you have a funeral for a baby that small? It seems heartless not to but it seems cruel to put Janie and Bryan through that. To have to talk to people and explain what happened. People always say the wrong thing, you can have another, but now she can't. I can't imagine Janie without a baby on her hip. That girl was born to mother the world." He looked at Jeanie.

"How are you feeling?" I could see Todd was concerned for Jeanie, they had been trying for so long and to have your sisters pregnancy end like this, it was taking a toll on both of them

"I'm beat, I don't know about everyone else, but I just want to sleep. Jeanie, you guys go home, we'll stay since the boys are here. Come over in the morning so we can pull the house together for Janie before Bryan brings her home."

"Are you sure? We can stay, they have the pull out couch downstairs."

"Go, we are going to sleep on the pull out couch. Janie's bed has to be stripped before anyone can sleep in there. Scott said he pulled the comforter up to hide the blood from the kids so no one can sleep in there tonight."

Todd and Jeanie hugged us and headed out, with Jeanie promising to return in the morning before any of the kids woke up.

After they left I turned to Scott, wishing things were different and I could curl up in his arms and break down. "I'll get the sleep sofa ready so you can go to sleep, then I'll strip the bed so I can try to soak the stains out of the sheets."

"I'm not staying here. I think I've spent enough time with your sisters kids and in this disaster she and Bryan call a home. I'm sleeping in my bed tonight. Make sure the boys stick to their schedule." With that, Scott turned and headed out the door.

After Scott left I sat on the couch and cried. I cried until there was nothing left. I paced the floor and talked to myself. I ranted at the world, doctors, hospitals, God, and the twisted fate that allowed this to happen to my baby sister. I didn't know how I could fix this, how to make things okay again. Nothing would never be okay. Things would return to normal, but forever, Janie will have lost Lily. Nothing can make that okay.

I fell asleep on the couch, too worn out to even make up the bed. When I woke up a few hours later, I got up and checked on the kids, Lacey had wet the bed but the rest were sleeping peacefully. I changed Lacey and tucked her on the couch. I climbed back on the couch, said a silent prayer for all that was right in the world, and drifted off.

What's next

"So, what are you thinking?" Todd asked when we got in the car. "Besides the fact that life is so unfair."

"I don't know, right now I'm so all over the place. Yesterday all day, I kept thinking about how I would approach my sisters with the surrogate idea, if we decided to go down that road, now that seems so petty and self-absorbed."

"Yesterday you didn't know any of this. The last thing anyone could accuse you of is being self-absorbed." Todd took his hand off the wheel to hold mine.

"It was horrible, Todd. I can't even begin to describe how horrible it was. Initially when no one would tell us what was going on with Janie and they shoved Bryan out of the room and rushed her off to surgery, I was terrified. I felt like I couldn't breathe, no one would tell us anything and Bryan either didn't know or was just too emotional to talk about it. Waiting for that doctor seemed like years. I thought that was the worst thing that could ever happen. But then the doctor came in and I found out that I had no idea, really, what the worse thing in the world was. Now I know, it's a baby dying. I still cannot fathom that she died. How does a baby die? Why does a baby die? In all our struggles with infertility, it never crossed my mind that being infertile might not be the worst thing that could happen. I never, ever thought about losing a baby."

"Of course you didn't, neither did Janie. It sounds like this was a freak thing, not something that anyone could have anticipated. Are you sure you're okay? I know it had to be hard for you to hold that baby, today of all days." Todd was concerned, but he didn't understand, he was still thinking about our IVF cycle and the possible outcome. We had been down this road too many times to get our hopes up.

"Funny thing is, I totally forgot that today was the big day, and when I remembered it didn't seem all that important anymore. I don't know if I can do the surrogate thing, after this. I'm not sure I can ask someone to take that risk for me."

Todd stopped for a red light and glanced over at me, "We don't have to decide this tonight, we don't even have to talk about it. Maybe we never have to talk about it. Did the doctor call today?"

"I don't even know, we turned our phones off last night and only turned them on to take pictures of the baby. I'm sure there is a message but it will still be there tomorrow. Tonight, I can't deal with it."

"Let's just focus on Janie and Bryan. Whatever happens, happens."

That's why I love this man so much, he always knows what I need to hear, but at this point I'm not sure I'll ever want to talk about getting pregnant again.

I slept like a rock, my bed is so much more comfortable than a hospital chair and when I heard Todd get up I just wanted to stay in the cocoon of my blankets. I knew, however, that my ever efficient sister would be up before the sun, cleaning, cooking, doing laundry, hell she might even paint the fence! Julie would make sure that Janie did not have to worry about anything when she got home today. Not that Janie cared, she lived her life for those little people and if the house was messy and the only clean clothes they had were pajamas, Janie didn't care. She just wanted to enjoy her babies.

I rolled out of bed and headed to the bathroom. I climbed in the shower with Todd, this was my favorite part of waking up, both of us still half asleep, waking up under the warm spray of the shower. When Todd went out to mow the yard I was still in my robe, "Call if you need anything. I have tons to do in the yard but I'll keep my phone with me." He kissed me and headed out the door.

I finished getting ready and drove to Janie's. My prediction had been correct, every light was on in the main floor of the house and when I opened the door and walked in, I could hear the vacuum. I almost laughed. Julie is so predictable, I could see her making a list in her head when we walked in last night.

I put my purse on the kitchen table and walked in the front room to let Julie know I was there. My sister was standing in the middle of the room the vacuum running, crying. “Hey Sister, are you ok?” I put my arm around her.

“I'm fine, just weepy this morning. I took some toys downstairs and found the baby boxes that Janie must have recently pulled out for the new baby. I stuck them back under that stairs, I didn't want her to have to see them.”

“Wow, there's really no way to keep this from sneaking up on you is there? And if it's this hard for us, what are the next few months going to be like for Janie?”

“I know, my heart is breaking for her. I called the hospital and talked to Bryan, he said she didn't sleep very well, she kept crying in her sleep and waking herself up. The doctor said if everything looks good she will be released by eleven. Want some coffee? I made a fresh pot, we might as well take a minute to enjoy the quiet before the kids get up.”

We settled into Janie's kitchen, repeating the movements we had done so many times over the last six years when the three of us had sat down to talk and share our day to day lives. I thought about all the babies that had been conceived at this table. Of course not actually conceived but conceived in the minds of their mothers and aunts.

Babies were always a huge topic of conversation. Each time one of my sisters decided to have a baby, we talked about it around this table. When Julie's twins were conceived, we got to know them around this table, before they were ever born. Through Julie, Janie and I learned what it was like to be pregnant. Your sister shares the things with you that no one really talks about, the increased sex drive, the hemorrhoids, the times you wet your pants from a well-placed kick, learning how to still have sex, comfortably around a growing baby.

Each time we went through IVF I told my sisters the details, around this table, and each time we hoped and prayed and they said "This is your turn." Each disappointment was discussed around this table too.

Would there be no more babies? Julie was done, ever efficient Julie, got her two kids in one fell swoop and was done with the whole baby making business. I couldn't seem to get started and now Janie was done. Julie and I had joked with Janie about Michelle Duggar being her hero. Janie was so in love with each of her babies and said she and Bryan wanted six but she didn't know that she would be done at six. Each pregnancy, birth, and new baby were such a joy for Janie, and she reveled in it. Would she be okay now?

“I was just thinking about babies, how much of our lives revolved around our ability or inability to have babies.” Julie got up to get more coffee. “I'm sorry sister, I know this is hard for you. I keep hoping that there are somehow, somewhere, more babies in our future.”

At that moment I wanted to tell Julie about my most recent cycle, but I couldn't. I didn't want to give her a glimmer of hope just to immediately dash it. I had listened to the message from Dr. Garcia's office, they asked me to call back, but I had no reason to believe it would be happy news. How can I feel sorry for myself and grieve for what will never be when Janie just lost a baby? And what if it was good news? How do I celebrate a new life when the rest of my family is grieving? Instead of telling Julie, I rinsed my coffee cup out and started unloading the dishwasher.

"Sister, there's something you're not telling me." Julie knows me too well. I close the dishwasher and turn to her.

"No, I'm just lost in my head over all of this. Let's go get Janie's room done before the kids wake up. If it's as bad as the guys say, we don't want the kids to see that."

Janie's home

Jeanie and I worked through the morning, mostly in shifts. The kids all started waking up right after we had stripped Janie's bed and remade it. I went into the kitchen to start breakfast while Jeanie was downstairs in the laundry room putting the sheets in to soak.

The kids were full of energy, I think Janie's kids were more than a little stressed, they didn't know what was going on. They just wanted their Mommy and Daddy. The girls were whinier than usual and even Collin, sweet, even tempered Collin seemed to find fault with everyone and everything.

After my boys managed to knock their cereal bowls off the table while fighting over who got to sit next to Porter, I decided everyone needed some outside time.

Jeanie dressed the kids and sent them out to the yard. She kept the baby in the house with her while she did laundry and cleaned the bathrooms. The day had a surreal quality to it. It wasn't often that Jeanie and I were both home and could play games with the kids and just be silly with them.

At eleven, Bryan called to say Janie was being released. He was going to take her to lunch because he was hoping the kids would be napping when they got home so Janie would have a minute to settle in before the kids realized she was there.

We told him to take his time and taught the kids to play freeze tag and then we did several rounds of mother may I, followed by parading around the yard acting like circus animals. We were hoping to wear everyone out so naps would be long.

The kids had been asleep for about fifteen minutes when Bryan and Janie pulled in. I put on a fresh pot of coffee and Jeanie got Janie's favorite blanket off the couch.

My poor baby sister, she walked so slowly and looked so defeated. Her face was still red and swollen from crying. Janie walked into the kitchen and looked around.

"Where are the kids?"

"They just went down for their naps, we've been playing in the yard all day. Porter learned how to pretend to be an elephant." Jeanie told her with a smile, "Come sit down, I have your blankie, and Julie just made fresh coffee."

"In minute, I want to see my babies." She headed down the hallway to the stairs, with Bryan right behind her. Jeanie and I waited in the kitchen, unsure if she needed us or if she just needed a moment to reassure herself that her life was exactly as she left it.

After a bit Janie and Bryan came into the kitchen. Janie settled in a chair and took the cup of coffee I made for her.

"How are you feeling? Are you in any pain?" I wasn't sure how you would feel after a hysterectomy but I was sure it couldn't be good, or pain free.

"Physically, I feel okay. My stomach is tender and I'm still nauseous but overall, I feel fine. I just can't believe this happened. I must have made Dr. Merrill tell me ten times what happened. It's like it won't sink in. And I keep forgetting. We were sitting at lunch and Bryan and I were talking about the kids and I suddenly thought, I don't think I've felt the baby kick this morning. Then I remembered, I'm never going to feel her kick again." Janie's eyes filled with tears but she held herself together.

We sat quietly in the kitchen. Bryan had gone into the garage to do whatever men do in the garage. I think he just needed to be alone with his grief.

"How did Porter sleep last night? Has he had his antibiotic? It feels like I've been away from the kids for a month."

“He slept fine. We started his medicine this morning when he woke up, of course no one remembered with everything going on. I stayed with the kids last night and never heard a peep until about 4am. Lacey wet the bed.”

“Oh my sweet little girl, she has been doing so well staying dry. I bet she was sad.”

“She was still half asleep so I just cleaned her up, stripped the bed, and put her back to bed with me. First thing this morning I remade her bed and tucked her back in it. She was her usual smiling self when she came down to breakfast.”

“Thank you both so much, I knew I didn't have to worry about the kids and that made it easier to stay in the hospital and do what had to be done. They asked us what we wanted to do with her. I know they have to ask, but it just seemed so cold. Bryan and I decided we don’t want a funeral or anything like that, we will just have her buried next to Gram and Pop, we have the plot they bought for Mom but we didn't use because she wanted to be cremated. You guys don't mind do you?”

“Of course we don't mind, right Jeanie? I never really gave that plot any thought, I didn't think we would ever need it. I'm just glad it’s there, one less thing for you to have to worry about.”

The three of us looked at the ceiling at the same time, we heard the first of the little feet hitting the floor and heading for the bathroom.

“Someone's up,” Jeanie said, “Have you decided when and how you want to tell the kids?”

“I thought… I guess I didn’t really think about it. Only Collin will really understand. Lacey may a little, but Brie and Porter are too young. By next week they will have forgotten that there was going to be another baby.” Janie looked at Julie, “Do you want me to tell your boys so I can answer their questions?”

“Oh sweetie, I can do that, it will be hard enough to tell Collin.”

“It's okay, I think it might be good for them to hear it from me, to understand what happened so the next time someone is pregnant they won't be afraid.” Janie looked at Jeanie and smiled.

Sam came around the corner, Max wasn't far behind, and Collin was trailing him. “There are my handsome nephews.” Jeanie said, scooping up Max. Collin ran straight for Janie.

“Mommy! I was so happy when Aunt Julie said you would be home, I missed you for days!” Janie leaned over to squeeze Collin in a tight hug.

“Oh my little man, I missed you even more than that, I think I missed you for years!” Collin tried to climb up in Janie's lap, I started to reach for him but Janie shook her head. “Hey big guy, you can't sit on Mommy's lap for a little bit because my tummy hurts.”

“You were bleeding, right Mommy? So you had to go to the hospital so the doctor could make you better. Did he give you a bandaid for your boo boo?”

Janie laughed, “Yes, he did Collin, right across my tummy.”

“Did he get our baby out? Bryson said his sister popped right out of his Mommy's tummy but I told him that you and Daddy said babies come out of the birth candle.”

Janie was very forthright with her children, she always told them the truth in language they could understand. I wonder what Collin thought a birth candle looked like.

“It's actually called a birth canal, big guy, but sometimes babies do come out of their Mommies tummies instead.” Janie looked at me over Collin's head. I glanced at my boys, cuddling with Jeanie and back at Janie, I nodded my head slightly. “And yes, the doctor got our baby out of my tummy.”

At this, all three boys perked up. Around here, a new baby was almost as fun as a puppy and they wanted to see this one. “Where is he? Did I get a brother? Oh, Mommy I wanted another brother, Porter's kind of a crybaby. Did we get a baby that's not a crybaby? I want to see him, where is he?"

I could see Janie struggling, "We got a sister this time Collin, but I'm afraid you can't see her. Remember when we talked about how sometimes people die and go to Heaven and wait for us?" Collin nodded his little head," That's where your sister is sweetie, it just wasn't her time to be born so when I got sick and the doctor had to take her out of my tummy, she wasn't ready yet so she had to go to Heaven."

"Where's Heaven? Can we go play with her when she's ready to be born?'

"No baby, we won't see her for a very long time, but we took lots and lots of pictures before she had to leave, and I think she was very sad that she couldn't come and play with you guys."

I looked at my boys, they were watching Janie intently but I could tell they didn't really understand. They were confused each time Janie had a baby, first the baby was in her belly then the baby was here. Now the baby wasn't in her belly but it also wasn't here. We were not a religious family, our grandparents had been religious but not active church goers and none of us had ever taken our kids so the concept of Heaven was hard for them to understand.

"Is there anything you want to know? Any questions you have?" Janie looked at the three boys, they all shook their heads but then Sam piped up and said, "Next time will you get us a brother, Aunt Janie? But wait until he's ready to be borned." Then the boys ran out of the room to play in the family room.

"I'm so sorry Janie, he doesn't understand." I was devastated that Sam had brought up the one thing we were all avoiding.

"Of course he doesn't know, he just likes babies." Then she looked at Jeanie and smiled that Janie smile that she uses when she thinks she knows something you don't, "I guess Aunt Jeanie will just have to get them a brother."

“Don't even go there, the odds are better that Julie will have the next baby than me.” Jeanie put her cup in the sink as Bryan came into the kitchen.

“I guess I should round up the boys so you guys can settle in, I think it’s going to be another long night.”

“I can't believe I'm still tired, “Janie said, “I think all I did at the hospital was sleep.”

“Not very well though,” Bryan said, rubbing her back.

Jeanie and I got ready to go and we heard the rest of the kids start to stir upstairs. I went and got the girls while Jeanie took Porter to Bryan. Porter saw Janie and about turned himself inside out to get to her. Bryan was trying to explain that Mommy's tummy hurt but neither Porter nor Janie would have any of that.

"Give me that handsome boy of mine," Janie said smiling at Porter. She snuggled him on her lap and kissed his head. "I missed you so much baby boy."

I gathered the boys, hugged everyone, and headed out to the car with Jeanie close behind. We had promised Janie and Bryan we would be back first thing in the morning, but told them to call if they needed anything before that.

An unusual voicemail

The rest of the week passed quickly. Julie and I went to Janie's every day. It was kind of nice to hang out with my sisters and the kids every day with no agenda. The hardest day was the day we buried Lily. Julie lined up a sitter for all six of the kids and it was just us and our husbands. Well, except Scott, he had to go back to Nebraska. One of Janie's neighbors was a pastor at a local church and Bryan asked him to say a few words over the baby. In less than an hour, Lily had been laid to rest.

Janie held up surprisingly well. I think having four other kids who had no idea Mommy just wanted to climb in bed and pull the blankets over her head had helped. Porter had been super clingy since Janie came home from the hospital, and Lacey was put back into diapers because she seemed to forget that she was potty trained. Losing Lily had an effect on Janie's kids even though they didn't realize and couldn't verbalize it.

I went back to work the following week and was quickly swept up in all that had piled up on my desk while I was gone. I had, for the most part, forgotten about my test results. I had pushed it to the back of my mind after listening to the message from the doctor's office and didn't think about it again.

The week I spent with Janie I made it very clear to Todd that I didn't want to talk about it, he respected my wishes, although I know it was hard for him. I wasn't ready, wasn't sure when I would be ready and had just decided to let my period clear things up for me. I knew it would come, like it always had, when it was ready. When Todd and I first started trying to have a baby that was the most frustrating thing, my period had never been regular, and even thought I knew that, when the normal twenty eight days had passed, my hopes would start to rise. Usually I went and bought a pregnancy test, just to be disappointed. Now, I was just going to let my body do what it did best. I didn't want to think about it, I didn't want to worry about it. I was positive my period would come and there would be no need to hear the disappointment in the nurse's voice when I called for my test results.

It had been two weeks since Janie lost the baby but so much had happened that when Friday rolled around I was exhausted. I just wanted to go home and curl up with a good book and a glass of wine. Friday is Todd's poker night so I knew he would pick up dinner on his way home from work, so I wouldn't have to cook. We would eat, and he would be gone until eleven or so, depending on how the game was going. I was definitely looking forward to this night.

I almost made it out of my office when my phone rang, I debated answering it but decided to let it go to voicemail. Whatever it was could wait until Monday.

Todd had stopped at our favorite Italian place, I saw the bag on the counter when I came in. I walked in to the dining room, Todd was in the process of serving up our dinner. I always got their crab stuffed ravioli in a sun dried tomato Alfredo sauce, it was amazing. Todd got the seafood linguine. The dining room smelled heavenly. I grabbed a breadstick and headed to the pantry to get a bottle of wine. We had a little wine cooler that fit right under the shelves in the pantry, I grabbed a red, two glasses and the cork screw from the kitchen and went back into the dining room.

Todd was in a hurry, he had skipped the last two weeks and was anxious to hang out with the guys. I was glad because I was so tired I could barely hold up my end of the conversation.

"Leave the dishes hon, I'll get them when I get home. You look beat." Todd was putting the dishes in the sink, walking back and forth to clear the table.

"I think everything is finally catching up with me. I was looking forward to reading tonight but I think I'll be asleep before you are out of the driveway." I walked into the kitchen to get my purse off the table. I had heard my phone vibrate several times during the day but hadn't had a chance to check it.

I had a voice mail so I hit the button to retrieve it while Todd was grabbing his jacket. He came into the kitchen to kiss me goodbye.

"Jeanie? Hey, what's going on? Is everything okay?" Todd was looking at me, but I couldn't speak. "Jeanie, say something, what the hell is going on?"

I had finished listening to the message, I hit five to replay it and put the phone on speaker.

"Hi Jeanie, it's Lisa from Dr. Garcia's. I'm calling about your ultrasound, I don't see you on the schedule so I wanted to make sure you got on the calendar before we were booked up."

"What? What does that mean? Play it again." Todd looked as confused as I felt. After the message played again, he looked at me. "What does that mean? What ultrasound? Is everything okay? You are really freaking me out."

I sat down in the kitchen chair. “Remember I had my blood work done the day Lily died? They left a message for me to call for my results. I never called, Todd.” I looked at him and took his hand. “I don't know, I might be wrong, but this has never happened before. Honey, I think I'm pregnant, I think it worked. The ultrasound is the last step before they release you to your obstetrician. We've never had this happen before. Oh my God, I think I'm pregnant.”

“Are you sure? Is there any other reason for an ultrasound? Call them back.”

“No, I'm not sure. I don't know, I just know that every other time, the result was negative, I got my period and we moved on.” I looked at the clock on the kitchen wall, “It’s after six, I would just get the answering service and this isn't really an emergency.”

“So we wait until Monday? Are you kidding me?” Todd ran his hand through his hair. “We have to know, as much as I want to believe that this time, finally it worked, I'm scared Jeanie. What if you're not pregnant but they saw something else in your blood work?”

“I don't think they tested my blood for anything else. Monday will have to be soon enough”

“Wait, can't you get a pregnancy test? That would let us know, I would feel better then. I'll run to Walgreens and...”

“No, you are going to play poker and I am going to sleep. Todd, whatever it is, there is nothing we can do about it right this minute, or even in the next few days.”

“It will only take about twenty minutes.”

I interrupted him again, “Seriously Todd, I don't want to have this conversation, I don't want to take a pregnancy test, I just want to go to sleep. Go, get out, have fun, win lots of money, and be careful. I love you, honey, but I'm too tired to deal with this.”

Todd protested a bit more, I just leaned again the door jamb and yawned. Eventually he gave up, kissed me, and headed out the door. I went into the kitchen, rinsed the dishes and put them in the dishwasher.

I briefly thought about taking a bath but finally, the call of my pillow was too much so I washed my face, brushed my teeth and went to sleep. I didn't stir when Todd came in and put the pregnancy test on my nightstand.

Trying to get back to myself

“Mommy, can we have pancakes this morning? I'm don't want more cereal.” Collin was laying on the bed next to me, trying to wake me up. It used to be, I got up with Bryan so I had a little time in the morning before the kids woke up. I loved watching them wake up. Since Lily died, Collin and the girls were up and ready to start their day before my eyes were open. They would finally wake me up when Porter woke up.

I rolled onto my back. Mornings were no longer my favorite time of day. Every morning for thirty seconds or so, I forgot. Then it would come rushing back. It was like reliving it over and over again. Everything I had heard or read said it would get easier. I can't believe it. How does it ever get easier to have a baby in the ground instead of in your arms?

“Alright you sleepyheads, I can't believe you have been sleeping the whole day away.” I smiled at the kids. “Let me get Porter up and changed. I have an idea, how about we all get dressed and go to IHop for breakfast?

The kids squealed and ran out of the room. I knew Brie would need help but Collin and Lacey were pros at dressing themselves. I went down the hall, I could hear Porter calling my name, and it made me smile. I didn't really want to go out but I thought I should get the kids out of the house, it isn't fair to them that I want to become a hermit.

I picked up my baby, my last baby, ever, and held him to me. I must have been holding him a little tightly because Porter started to protest and pushed against me. He wanted to be put down so he could charge down the hall and find the other kids. I grabbed a clean diaper and an outfit for the day. I quickly got Porter changed and dressed, noticing that his clothes were getting a little small. Already my baby boy was outgrowing his eighteen month clothes. I will never again have a baby to wear these clothes.

Every day I am reminded there will be no more babies. Somedays I'm not sure which is worse, Lily dying or never being able to have another baby. Friday will be three weeks since Lily died, three weeks since the course of the rest of my life changed. I don't know what to do about it, all I know is I want that life back, I want Lily and all the rest of my yet to be born babies back.

I put Porter down and go to find Brie, at two and a half she was asserting her independence. She wanted to be able to do everything on her own and was becoming increasingly frustrated by her inability to keep up with her siblings. When I went into her room I was able to avert a meltdown. Lacey had gotten the dress Brie wanted from the closet and Brie was starting to make her little fuming noises because she could not get the dress over her head. I reached down and unbuttoned the two buttons on the shoulder that were keeping it from slipping on and Brie's little face popped out of the dress. She looked so proud.

"I do it Mommy. CeeCee pull it down." I buttoned those two buttons back up and got a clean diaper for her. Brie was not at all interested in potty training, although she was very interested in her sister's big girl panties and, as usual, she had a pair on over her diaper. I finished up with Brie and heard the other three heading downstairs,

Collin patiently helping Porter. Sometimes it was hard to believe he wasn't even five yet.

I went into my room, threw on a pair of jeans, quickly washed my face, brushed my teeth and ran a brush thought my hair, I tried hard not to look at myself, I didn't want to see Lily's death etched on my face. Today, I need to take care of the babies I have.

"Okay, my little chickadees, who wants pancakes!" I said coming into the kitchen. Three little people started jumping up and down, Porter saw them and started doing a little hop. At times like these I wondered why I couldn't be more grateful for what I have.

About twenty minutes and the rounding up of eight shoes later, we were laced, velcroed and buckled into the van. I drove down the street, remembering the last time I had been out of the house was to bury Lily. I pushed that thought away and tried to focus on this day, my babies singing in their car seats, the sun warming my face.

Taking four kids under five anywhere is always an adventure. It also always gets you noticed. This morning when I had the brilliant idea of taking my brood for pancakes, I forgot the waitresses at IHop know us, they knew about the baby on the way. After ten minutes I was counting the seconds until we could leave. The waitress, Ginny, waited on me and the kids all the time. She commented how good I looked for being pregnant and said the kids must keep me thin. I wanted to hit her. Then a neighbor from down the street came in with her boys, she just had to stop by the table and tell me how sorry she was, before trying to arrange a playdate for our kids. I had to tell her I would get back to her.

It was too loud in there, the kids were misbehaving, Lacey was whining, then Brie was crying, Porter threw his drink. I felt so close to screaming. I was absolutely out of control. Ginny came by our table and I stood up and told her I was going to be sick. “Can you keep an eye on them for just a second, I'll be right back.” Before she could answer I ran to the bathroom. I sat in a stall and sobbed, why did I think I could pretend everything was normal? Why did I go out without Bryan? I started to be afraid that I couldn't get the kids home.

Ginny came into the bathroom. She is in her fifties and the sweetest lady. “Are you okay, what can I do?”

I just cried harder. I didn't want to leave the bathroom, I felt like everyone was staring at me, whispering about the baby I had lost. Ginny put her arm around me, “Honey, when you came in here your neighbor noticed how upset you were and told me about the baby. I'm so sorry, I didn't mean to be so insensitive when you came in. I lost my son when he was two days old. That was over twenty years ago, some days it's still so raw.” She put her arms around me. “You cry all you want, I can keep those babies of yours busy until you feel better. I'm actually off in about twenty minutes so I can help you with them.”

Just when you thought the world was a cold, lonely place, someone comes along who understands exactly. I was so grateful to Ginny. After a few more minutes I was able to pull myself together and go back to the kids. Only Collin seemed to notice my red face and swollen eyes, he came over next to me, gave me a hug and went back to his pancakes. My little boy is going to be one hell of a man one day.

True to her word, when Ginny's shift was over she grabbed a cup of coffee and came and sat with me and the kids. We talked about babies and kids and pancakes.

When we were finished Ginny followed me home, I told her it wasn't necessary, that I was okay now and when I got home I could put a video in for the kids and buy some time until they went down for their naps. She wouldn't hear of it, so she came home with us.

We settled the kids in front of a video then Ginny made a pot of coffee.

“Do you want to talk about it? I know when Mikey died some days it helped to talk, some days it didn't. So if you want to talk, I would love to listen. If not, we can just sit and maybe I can talk. Sometimes it feels like everyone has forgotten him so it's good to talk about him.”

“I would love to hear about him. But I want to know everything. I want to hear about when you carried him and when he was born.” I looked at Ginny, hoping she wouldn't think that was too personal.

"Let's see" Ginny stared over my shoulder. I was twenty five when I got pregnant with Mikey, his Daddy and I had been married for six years and had two little girls, we wanted a boy in the worst way. Thirty years ago ultrasounds weren't as common as they are now, they were used more if there was an emergency, not like today when they give you one so you know what you're having. I was sure Mikey was a girl, his Daddy was sure this was his boy. I remember saying, "I'm carrying this baby exactly like the other two, not one bit of difference so unless that little penis pops out the last day, I think we are getting another girl." Ginny took a drink of her coffee.

"When I was seven months pregnant with Mikey I went into labor. Now, after two babies, you know what labor is but I still tried to convince myself that wasn't the case. Both my girls were late, it was much too early. I spent the day with the worst backache and when my husband came home I asked him to take care of the girls so I could get in the tub. I had back labor with my girls too but I was still trying to convince myself it was just a backache. I ran a tub of water and sunk down in it. I had the lights off and a few candles lit so I could relax. I remember I was laying back with my eyes closed and I felt a rush of water leave my body. I opened my eyes and even in the dark I could see the blood. I called Bob to come help me. He saw the blood and picked me up, naked as the day I was born, grabbing my robe off the door and headed out the door with me. I don't know what he was thinking about the girls but fortunately when he was carrying me to the car the woman next door was coming out of her house to check the mail. She had been a friend to us since we lived there. Bob told her something was wrong and that Melanie and Tammy were still at the dinner table. She told him to go, get me to the hospital and she would take care of the girls. And she did, too, for most of the next two weeks.

"When we go to the hospital Bobby carried me in, he left the car right there in front of the hospital, still running. I don't know who ever moved it because I don't remember him leaving me, even when they said he had to, he held on tight and wouldn't let them make him go.

The doctor examined me and said the baby was crowning. Now this was just the hospital doctor on call, I was crying, trying to tell him that the baby couldn't be crowning, it wasn't time. But as you and I both know, when a baby says it's time, there's no stopping the little stinker.

“We didn't make it out of that exam room, Mikey was born seven minutes after we got to the hospital. He was so small, only a little over two pounds, the nursery team came in and they took him away. I didn't really get to see him. They tried everything but he had been deprived of oxygen and the trip through the birth canal was too much for him. The doctors did everything they could.”

I couldn't speak, I just sat there, quietly crying while she finished her story.

“When Mikey was thirty six hours old they said the machines were keeping him alive, he didn't have any brain function. They asked us for permission to turn off the machines. As you can imagine, the hardest thing in the world was to turn off those machines. Who wants to believe that their baby is dead, their beautiful, perfect little boy? We waited a few hours for the family to gather and then we told them to unhook him. The nurses unhooked all his wires and cords and tubes and I got to hold my baby boy for the first and only time. He was a strong baby and somehow he managed to keep breathing until his Daddy and all of his grandparents got to hold him too. Bob handed him back to me, I was sitting in a rocking chair, I kissed his little cheek and I heard a little breath, like a sigh, and he was gone."

Ginny got up to get more coffee. "Mikey was the only son I ever had. After he died Bob and I tried three more times, each time we got a beautiful daughter but there were no more sons for us. Now I have all grandsons so I guess things have a way of evening out."

"Oh Ginny, I didn't know, I'm so sorry. I don't know what to say."

"Oh honey, there is nothing to say, as you know. People who haven't lost a baby will try to say the "right" thing. They will tell you God had other plans for your baby, it wasn't his time, better to lose him early than later, God doesn't give you a cross too heavy to bear. It's all horseshit, there is nothing to say, and absolutely nothing anyone can say can make something so wrong, right. People just need to say, I'm sorry for your loss. There's nothing else."

"I'm finding that out. My sisters try to hard not to say the wrong thing so they don't say anything at all, but sometimes, I want to talk about her, I want to rant, and rave and scream about how wrong this is, but I feel like I can't. That's not what everyone wants to hear."

From the playroom Porter starts crying, I look at the clock and see it's naptime for the little guy. Ginny helps me get the kids down for their naps, they had such a late breakfast they can have lunch when they get up. Collin has pretty much outgrown his nap but the rule is you can read in bed until the others start to wake up, somedays Mommy needs naptime more than the kids do.

When I come back downstairs Ginny has made us lunch and poured glasses of tea. "If you'd like to talk about her, I'd love to hear her story."

I wasn't sure I could talk about Lily, but talk I did. For almost two hours I talked and cried, crying so hard sometimes that I couldn't talk because I couldn't breathe. Trying so hard to put into words what was inside of me. I was so angry, so scared, so hurt, and I wanted my baby back. Finally when I thought there were no more tears and no more words, I cried and told her I couldn't have any more babies. Ginny sat there, holding my hand, giving me more tissues, listening.

When I could say no more, Ginny spoke, "Most people don't understand this but for me the worst part was that my body had betrayed me. My body, which I trusted to keep my baby safe, had failed me. I couldn't blame the doctor or God or a car accident, this was my body that had pushed my boy into the world before his time and caused him to die. That was so hard for me."

"I know, I don't understand how this happened, why this happened. The doctor said there are no warning signs and nothing in my history showed a high risk for any complications." I was sobbing again.

Ginny rubbed my arm, "You know, I think most people either don't know or don't remember, but as a mother, as soon as you have a positive test, you think- my baby. This isn't a lump of cells, or a fetus, it's a person, your little person, and you would give your life for it from day one. Then the day comes when nothing you do, nothing you say, no matter how much you love or what promises you make to God, you can't help your child. That is the most devastating thing. I felt I had failed as Mikey's mom and no matter what anyone said, it was all my fault."

"Yes, yes, exactly," I said between sobs. "I didn't take care of Lily, I didn't save her, and now she is gone. I feel like I don't deserve to be a mother to the others because I failed their sister."

I just cried, there was nothing more to say and Ginny let me cry until my babies started waking up. "I guess I should get out of your hair." She gave me a hug. "Honey, those babies upstairs are yours for a reason. They love you, and you love them. There are no guarantees, we just have to love the ones we have and do the best we can. I wish I could tell you something that would make it better, but I can't, there is nothing. The old saying goes, time heals all wounds, and it does, but that doesn't mean you ever forget or that it ever hurts less. It just means you learn to live with that hurt and you remember the joy, even though it was so very short lived. There is so much joy in knowing you carried a baby, try to remember that."

When Ginny left I went to get the kids up. Collin came running at me, he stopped short. I've been moody and in pain lately. Now I see that it has stopped my big boy from his exuberant gestures of affection, it has made him cautious. I squat down, throw open my arms, “Is that the best you got buddy?” Collin comes running, almost knocking me over with his hug. Yes, this joy is always there. In the middle of the pain, the joy of just loving my children, is always there.

Scott's ultimatum

I was dreading this night, this weekend, the next week. Scott was coming home and he was determined we were going to talk about moving. I had been putting him off since Lily died, telling him I was too emotional, Janie needed me, any excuse I could think of not to talk about moving.

Now he was going to be home for nine days. There would be no more avoiding the subject. I had been trying to come up with something, anything, to stop this from happening. Even if it was only a delay. I couldn't leave now, Jeanie was finally pregnant. No one else knew yet, but I didn't want to miss sharing her joy. I knew Scott would not think that was a good enough reason not to move.

My boys were building Legos in the living room when Scott pulled in. Here we go, I have to find a way out of this!

Scott came in pulling a suitcase and carrying his laptop bag. “Wait until you see the house I found.”

“Just one? I thought there were several you liked?” I said, before turning to the boys asking them to pick up the Legos before dinner.

“I had to make a decision, you wouldn’t talk about it or look at any of the links I sent so I put in an offer on a house today.” Scott looked into the living room to make sure the boys were picking up.

I sat down in a chair at the kitchen table. “Scott, that isn’t fair, this is going to be my home too. I would like to at least see a few before we make a decision.”

“You should have thought about that the past three weeks. I told you when I came home we were moving, then with all the drama with your sister, you wouldn’t even talk about it.”

“Drama? That wasn’t Janie being dramatic Scott. She lost her baby. I’m sorry if I’ve had other things on my mind than the plans you made without even consulting me." I was so angry at him. How could he be so callous?

"In case you've forgotten, I don't need to consult you. It's my income that supports this family and my job is moving. I tried to talk to you about it as a courtesy, but I don't need your consent or approval to buy a house and move my family." Scott's eyes were dark, I knew I was pushing him but I didn't care.

"Well, if I am part of your family then you do need my consent to move me across the country. How can you ask me to leave right now?" The timer on the oven went off, it was meatloaf night.

"Boys, wash up for dinner." I turned to Scott, "I don't want to talk about this right now. Can we just let the boys enjoy having you home?"

Scott didn't answer me but left the room to put his suitcase in the bedroom. The boys came in and once Scott was back we sat down to dinner.

Sam and Max were so excited to tell their father all the fun things they had been doing with their cousins. They thought it was wonderful that they got to spend so much time with them. Scott thought I was neglecting them by spending so much time with my sister. I didn't even have the energy to respond to his little digs about my parenting.

After dinner I cleaned up the kitchen while Scott played with the boys. Not that he actually played with them, it was more an interrogation. Scott would pull out a board game but while they played he would ask them about things they had done and what time they went to bed, and what they had for lunch. Did they listen to their mother, did they make their beds, and were they taking showers instead of baths. My poor boys, they didn't even realize they were being interrogated and that anything they said could and would be used against their mother.

I folded the dishtowel over the oven handle, sighed, and headed upstairs. I planned to be in bed and asleep before Scott came to bed. He always put the boys to bed the first night he was home so I had some time to get myself to bed before he came in. Tomorrow was our sister day so with any luck I could put off our talk until tomorrow night.

Scott woke up in a good mood, he was going to play golf with Todd and Bryan, and he loved beating them and then bragging about it.

I love these days with my sisters. Scott can't schedule them, so I can let the boys do what they want as long as they are ready for bed at bedtime. My sisters and I try to spend one Saturday a month just us and the kids. The men play golf, have a few drinks and dinner out. We also do one Saturday every few months that's just us girls. This was supposed to be that Saturday, but Janie doesn't want to leave the kids. I understand, but at the same time I look forward to that one day without the boys. Either way, today is our day. Janie has a day full of kid friendly activities planned. It will be exhausting but fun.

When I got to Janie's, Jeanie and Todd were already there talking to Janie and Bryan.

"Are you sure you don't want me to take the kids? You need some downtime." Bryan was saying to Janie.

"I already have everything planned, we are going to have fun. Go with the guys, get out, enjoy yourself, we'll be here when you get back." Janie said, kissing him on the cheek.

"I can tell where I'm not wanted." Bryan said picking Porter up. "Give me a kiss little man, Momma is banishing me from the house."

After the guys left we sent the kids into the family room to watch a movie. Sister day always started with coffee and gossip.

"I could have used a day without the boys, sister. I need some time to hear my own thoughts." I said to Janie after we got our coffee and settled around the table.

"That's because you need to learn to relax. Everything will be fine if you ignore your schedule, things will still get done, the boys will still be well behaved, and you will be less stressed."

"I need to be organized, I can't stand flying by the seat of my pants. It's just not in my nature. Besides, the boys do better with a schedule, they respond really well to structure." I was parroting to Janie and Jeanie the words Scott said to me all the time. The only difference is that he said I needed the schedule or my house would fall apart and the kids would never be fed.

"Sister, I love you but you have control issues. Let those boys be boys." Jeanie said sipping her coffee.

"So, sister, what's on the agenda today?" I asked Janie.

"I thought since the weather is so crappy we would make Christmas ornaments with the kids."

"Ornaments? It's only August, we have months to think about that." The thought of six kids, paint, glitter and glue was already making my head hurt.

"The kids all love when we do craft days. I made up some cinnamon dough and got the Christmas cookie cutters out. It will be fun, you know the boys will love it."

“You're right, they will, and they all make the cutest little things and they are so proud. I’m just not sure how many more handprint ornaments my tree can hold.” I said but I was laughing. Scott hated the ornaments the kids made, he wanted our tree to look like something out of a magazine. That made me love their wobbly, crumbly ornaments even more.

“Hey sister,” Janie said, turning to Jeanie, we haven’t talked about your options in a while. Have you and Todd decided what you want to do? Surrogate or adoption?”

Jeanie looked uncomfortable, “Well we really haven’t decided.” She snuck a look at me. I knew it was killing her not to tell Janie but she also didn’t want to tell Janie, not now.

“I'm glad that there are options like surrogacy, but I don’t know how those women do it. I mean, I get so attached while I'm pregnant, it would be so hard to come home from the hospital knowing your baby was going home with someone else.” Janie stopped for a minute and swallowed hard, “Although I guess it would have been easier than not coming home with Lily.”

“Oh, Janie, I'm so sorry, let’s not talk about this, not now.” Jeanie said, grabbing Janie's hand.

“No, it's okay. It's going to be hard to think about her for a while, but you know, I think the best thing has been talking about her. I made a new friend, at IHop of all places. She’s a waitress there and she lost her son when he was two days old. I’m sure other people would think it's morbid but she just lets me talk about Lily, she lets me scream and punch a pillow and be pissed off that this happened to me. But I also get to talk about how perfect she was, how tiny and new, and how nothing bad will ever happen to her. She won't skin her knee or knock her front tooth out, or get her heart broken. She will always be perfect.”

We heard the sounds of boredom from the other room so Janie got up to get the dough out of the fridge while Jeanie and I rounded up the troops. Janie had a basket full of Bryan's old shirts she saved for art projects and Jeanie and I got each little one into a shirt. Of course then they all paraded around the kitchen pretending to be their Daddies.

About two hours and lots of ornaments later, we finally had the last ones painted and waiting to dry. Janie took the girls upstairs to bath them and I took all the boys into the hall bath. Porter fell asleep sucking his thumb before we could get the paint off of him, Jeanie tucked him in his crib just the way he was and took a couple pictures of him.

We fed the kids lunch and tucked them into beds for naps. They were a little late today but that was okay, it was our sister day, there was no schedule, no rules. Although I did worry a little that the boys would not be ready for bed when bedtime came, but then I remembered they will be tuckered out from playing with their cousins so it should be okay.

Back downstairs we played some cards. My sisters and I were very competitive about our card games, and we had a ball laughing and teasing each other.

“Next time, let's go to Gardener Village and walk around while the guys have the kids. I love that place, but in the fall and winter it's a madhouse, you can't even walk around there. What do you think, we could go there and then get manicures and pedicures? It's been forever since we've done that.” It was my turn to deal.

“I don't think so,” Janie said, “I don’t know what it is, but since Lily died I don't want to leave the kids, even for a minute. I think it's making Bryan nuts because I've even been taking all four to the grocery store, which really is insane, but I just have this overwhelming fear of missing anything.”

“You will be a better mother if you take some time for yourself.” Jeanie said, “Well that's what all the parenting books I've read say. Don't look at me like that, just because I don't have kids doesn't mean I don’t know anything.”

“Sorry, I didn't mean to hurt your feelings it's just that you are the last person I would expect to lecture me about leaving my kids.” Janie said. “I know it doesn't make sense, I even know it's not rational, but right now, I'm not rational. I want to scoop my kids up and just hug them close to me and keep them safe. I don't want to miss one thing. Before, I noticed the things the kids did but I was always busy. Now I know, especially with Porter, this is the last time, there will be no more babies. I hate saying this but knowing that I will never again have a baby is almost harder than losing Lily."

"Sweetie, we don't know how you feel and we would never try to tell you what is right and what is wrong, we don't know. This is your grieving process and you have to do it your way. I just miss my sister time. You guys are my best friends and although it's always fun to get all the kids together I really, really love when it's just the three of us. But, until you are ready we will just enjoy naptime."

"Okay, next subject." Janie said, "I don't want to be sad all day."

"I've got a subject," Jeanie said, "How did you guys decide on your kids names? I know we've talked about it but I really want to know the story behind each one of them, including Lily. How do you know what a baby's name is before you've even seen it? Did you ever feel like you picked the wrong name for one of your kids?" I knew this was Jeanie's way of bringing up her pregnancy even though she wasn't ready to tell Janie yet.

"Scott picked the boys names. We talked about it for so long, I wanted something more modern and he wanted something traditional. After they cleaned the boys up and brought them into me, Scott handed each boy to me and told me his name. Samuel David and Maxwell Benjamin, they fit perfectly, and they were names I had vetoed earlier, but he was right, they are Sam and Max. I can't imagine calling them anything else. I had picked Drake and Brayden, can you imagine calling my boys by either of those names?"

"I always felt like my kids told me their names. I know it sounds silly but that's what it felt like to me. Bryan and I would make lists and read them off to each other every night. One by one we would find something wrong with them. I remember when Collin got his name, I just woke up one morning and was in the kitchen, he kicked really hard and I remember looking at Bryan and saying "Collin is active this morning." Bryan looked at me, looked at my belly, and agreed. Just like with Lily, we had that name on our list with Lacey but it was too old fashioned. In that room though, the name came to me out of nowhere. I like to think they name themselves if you let them."

"Hmmm, interesting. But what I'm really interested in is another croissant, are there any left?" Jeanie asked.

Janie said there were and Jeanie got herself one, I went to check on the kids, they were engrossed in The Sound Of Music. When I got back to the kitchen Janie and Jeanie were talking about labor.

"Ugh, I hate labor stories, they are all the same, it hurts so bad and then a little person pops out of your girlie bits and you thank God it's over. Don't romanticize it Janie, it's not pretty and it's not fun. It's messy and dirty and painful, and that's before the baby is born!" I said, I really did hate labor stories but I especially hated Janie's, they were somehow romantic and the way it should be, but I knew that is not always the case. I didn't want Jeanie to have false expectations. Janie was meant to give birth, she did it easily and she did it well.

“How come you never want to talk about when the boys were born? All women want to talk about their labor experience.” Jeanie said, “I would like to hear yours.”

“Oh God, do we have to do this? Okay, fine. Let's see, you know I was on bed rest the last several weeks, which was not any fun, “ I didn't tell them that Scott insisted that bed rest was not what I needed, I needed to be up doing the housework, then I could rest. “I started having contractions right after dinner, it was still a few weeks early so I thought they would stop. I got in the tub and tried to relax, but the boys had other plans. I don’t really remember much of it, which is what I don't understand about birth stories, I was in so much pain that everything is a blur. I remember getting to the hospital and being hooked up to all kinds of machines. I remember the neo natal team coming in because I was having twins and they were early. I remember it hurt, a lot. The epidural helped but by then I felt so out of control that nothing really helped. It felt like I pushed for days, Scott said it was about 45 minutes with Max and then ten minutes with Sam, but it felt like forever. What I do remember is my first glimpse of them. All slimy and red and screaming, they were the most beautiful things I had ever seen. And then I slept and slept and slept and I haven't slept since."

"Oh please, I think your boys slept through the night the day they came home from the hospital, they were the best babies." Janie said. I didn't have the heart to tell her it was because my infants were put on a strict schedule early on and quickly learned that no one came when you cried.

"Anyway, giving birth is different for everyone." I wanted to talk about anything but this. Luckily Porter needed to be changed and I shot Jeanie the evil eye for bringing up the labor stories.

The rest of the day passed quickly, six kids five and under have a way of making time fly. Before I realized it the guys were home, boasting about their golf game and the waitress who flirted with them.

We laughed and said we hoped they tipped her well if she had to put up with the three of them. Scott and I got the boys together, gave out tons of hugs and kisses, and were finally in the car on the way home.

"Did you boys have fun with your cousins?" Scott asked looking at the boys in the rearview mirror.

Both boys started talking at once, telling Scott about all the fun they had. I tuned them out, lost in my thoughts until Scott said, "After the boys are in bed, we need to talk. You can't keep avoiding this."

"You're right, it's time to sort this all out." That was all I said. I knew Scott thought that meant I had come to my senses but I had no intention of moving.

Sam and Max were exhausted so bedtime went quickly. I walked back into the family room where Scott was sitting on the couch with his laptop.

"Come and look at the house, it has everything we need."

"I'm not moving Scott. Not now. I need to be here for my sisters." I couldn't tell him Jeanie was pregnant, she had sworn me to secrecy until she told Janie.

“That’s ridiculous, your sisters always have something going on, some emergency. You can’t use them as an excuse not to move.” Scott was trying to keep his voice down because the boys were sleeping but I knew he was angry. I never stood up to him.

“I’m not using them as an excuse. I don’t want to move. It’s really not fair of you to just spring this on me and expect me to change my whole life. I won’t do it. The boys and I will stay here for a while.” I almost told him we would join him soon but I didn’t want to have him put a time limit on this.

“You can’t stay here. I told you I put an offer on another house. While I’m home this week, this one is going on the market. I can’t pay two mortgages. You and the boys will be with me.” Scott turned back to the computer screen signaling that he was done with this conversation.

“You don’t have to, I can pay the mortgage. You know I am making enough from my blog and writing for Moms of Many, I can afford it. The boys and I will stay here.” I swallowed hard.

After several minutes Scott looked at me. "You will not stay here, and neither will my children. We are moving, as a family, to Nebraska. There is nothing else to talk about."

I left the room and headed for the dining room. I had a blog post to edit and I wasn't going to let Scott see how shaken up I was.

We passed the rest of the time Scott was home barely speaking. If he talked to a realtor about the house, he never mentioned it. Several times he started to say something about when we were all in Nebraska but I just walked away. I wasn't going to discuss it with him.

I had never stood up to Scott. I let him dictate everything, right down to what we ate, but this was easier than I thought. I could also see that Scott was knocked off balance. Where was his docile wife and why wasn't she doing what he told her to?

Scott left and went back to Nebraska. Before he left he said with a smirk that he wanted my debit and credit cards as well as my checkbook. I grabbed my purse and handed them over to him without a word.

"We'll see how long you last. I'm serious Julie, I'm not giving you one penny. When you are ready to come to Nebraska, let me know." He grabbed his suitcase and headed to the Uber that was waiting at the curb.

Scott stayed true to his word. There was no money from him. I didn't need it and I even found the strength to refuse to discuss every detail of my day so he could judge me. He only came home every two months now and only for a weekend. Of course, I never knew when those weekends were, he was still trying to use the element of surprise to intimidate me.

I felt freer than I had in years. My boys were doing well, my writing was supporting us, and Jeanie was going to have a baby. I wish I had always known life could be this good.

Finally my turn

Everything is so new. I know it's not, women have been getting pregnant since the beginning of time, but to me, everything is new.

I went to the grocery store today and when I got to the diaper aisle, the one I usually avoid like the plague, I turned down it. It used to make me so angry that the tampons were in the same aisle with the diapers and wipes and lotions, now it made me smile because I remembered my secret, no tampons for me this time. This was the first time I had gone to the grocery store pregnant. The first time when I knew, absolutely knew, that I was going to be a mother.

I must have spent twenty minutes looking at everything. There's so much! How do you know what formula is right? I never imagined there was more than one. Diapers, diapers everywhere, so many brands and sizes and styles. I would need my sisters' help with that one. Oh, and the sweet smelling baby lotions. Janie's kids always smelled like baby lotion, even still, she says it's so relaxing for them to get a mini massage with lotion after their baths, that they fall asleep faster and sleep better. She still uses the baby lotion, even on Collin, she said she doesn't want to expose his skin to the harsher ingredients of adult lotions.

They even had a little section with socks and bibs and rattles. I picked up the tiniest pair of socks, white, just plain white, but soft as a whisper. I sat them on top of my purse in the cart. I wanted to buy more, some lotion maybe, start stocking up on diapers, but I felt like a novice at this, I definitely needed to ask my sisters some questions.

I walked through the store, a little smile playing on my lips. So happy that I wanted to tell everyone. I think that is the worst part about being in early pregnancy, no one can tell. I wanted to tell every person I made eye contact with at the store, everyone I talked to, but couldn't find a way to work it into the conversation.

I can't wait until people can look at me and see, see this wonderful little person that is keeping me company all the time. Does everyone feel like this? I know that not everyone does, sometimes being pregnant is not a good or happy thing and I can't imagine how horrible that must be, but for everyone else, is it always like this? Is each successive pregnancy just as magical as the first or is this the only time I will ever feel like this? I know we said this was the last time but now that I'm pregnant, that I know it will actually work, I am not willing to let someone else grow the rest of my embryos. Those babies, like this one, will grow under my heart.

When I got home Todd was already there. He came into the garage when he heard the door go up. I got out of the car and he kissed me.

“How are you feeling Mama?' he said with a smile.

“Better than I can even begin to tell you.” I opened the back door to get the grocery bags.

“Hey, that's my job, step away little lady, your knight in shining armor is here to save the day!”

I laughed and went to open the door between the house and garage. “I'm pregnant you know, not an invalid. Women have been working hard during pregnancy since Eve was in the garden. Carrying a grocery bag is not going to kill me.”

“That's what they say, but I say, why take chances? Besides, you better enjoy this pampering, once that baby is born, I expect to be waited on hand and foot.”

“Yes, I can see that happening now. I'll meet you at the door with your slippers and the newspaper. Oh wait, that's not me, that's the dog you are going to be sharing the doghouse with if you expect to be waited on!”

Todd laughed and set the grocery bags on the counter. “Come here woman,“ he said, wrapping his arms around me. “Tell me about your day, tell me everything.”

"Nothing special, just the usual. How did your day go?"

"That is not what I'm talking about, you are carrying the male heir to the kingdom with you all day, I want to know what the two of you do when I'm not watching."

"Oh, that. Well, first of all, we beheaded a couple of people, ordered others burned at the stake and, just for a change, we pardoned a couple people, and that was all before lunch."

"Seriously, were you okay? Did you feel alright, not sick or anything? I don't want you to work too hard or get stressed out. We don't need the money, we've been saving for years so that you could stay home when the time came."

"I'm fine honey, don't worry. I really can't even tell there is a baby there yet. I don't feel any different, maybe more tired than usual, but other than that, exactly the same. I'm amazed that I haven't even had any morning sickness. Don't worry, when the time comes, wild horses couldn't get me to leave this little one and go back to work. I've been looking forward to being a stay at home mom since we first started talking about having a family."

"You can't tell he's there? Really? I would think that if there is something growing in your belly you would feel it or something."

"I can't wait for that but most of the books I've read say that first time moms generally don't feel the baby move until around twenty weeks, some as early as sixteen but twenty is pretty normal. I'm gonna stick with twenty so I won't stress if I don't feel anything at sixteen."

"When are you gonna start showing? I can't wait to see that little bump and know it's my son in there."

"Wait a minute, what if it's your daughter? Will you still be excited?"

"Of course I will but I think we are having a boy. If you look at our siblings, every single one of them had a boy first, even my sister Lisa. She had a boy and then four girls, but the boy was first."

“I see your logic, although I don't know if that really has anything to do with it. Just so you know, I'm pretty positive this little one is a girl. We moms know these things.”

Todd laughed, “I don’t care, boy or girl, as long as it's healthy and happy and reasonably intelligent, what more can I ask for? Oh, and if she's a girl, I want her to look just like you.”

“Sweet talker. I'm starving. Let's feed this child, whatever it may be.”

Todd and I made dinner together and then I fell asleep on the couch watching a sitcom. When it was over Todd woke me up to go to bed. I brushed my teeth and went to the bathroom. These days going to the bathroom was the scariest thing I did. Every time I went I was so afraid there would be blood. I was relieved that there wasn’t and climbed in bed.

“Have you decided when you are going to tell Janie? It’s so hard to keep this a secret.” Todd asked, picking up a book from his nightstand.

“Tomorrow. I’m going to call and invite her to lunch and then I’ll tell her.” I kissed him quickly on the cheek and burrowed under the blankets. I was asleep before he even responded.

That night I dreamed of the baby for the first time. She was a chubby little girl with curly brown hair. I was in the tub with her giving her a bath and there were goldfish swimming in the tub with us. They say pregnant women have crazy dreams, I guess I know that's true now and not an old wives tale.

At work the next day I watched the clock. I kept putting off calling Janie but finally picked up the phone so she would have enough time to get the kids ready.

Janie answered the phone in her usual sing song way. “Hey sister of mine, I miss you.”

“I miss you too. Why don’t we take the kids out to lunch today? I’m missing the monkeys too.”

“When? The kids will be so excited. Collin, get Porter out of the dryer right now! Sorry, the kids are a little wired. When do you want to do lunch?”

Janie sounded great, the best I had heard her sound in a while. “How about today? I have a meeting at one but if we do lunch at eleven I can be back in time.”

“Perfect. The kids will be so excited to see you, we haven't seen you in over a week. What's up with that? Are you okay?”

“Yes, what are you doing worrying about me? Geez woman, sometimes I get busy and forget to stop by. Hence this phone call.”

Janie laughed. “Fair enough, where would you like to dine with my well behaved brood?” We ironed out the details. Jungle Jim's was not my idea of a good time but the kids could play and Janie and I could talk. I still had no idea how I was going to tell her I was pregnant. Talk about bad timing, I must be the poster child for that.

I'd known for sure, without a doubt, for almost a month and a half. The Saturday after Dr. Garcia's office called, when I woke up there was a pregnancy test on my nightstand. Todd bought it on his way home from the poker game. I didn't even notice at first, I got up, went to the bathroom and then climbed back in bed with my husband. He snuggled up to me and asked how I was feeling.

"Pretty wonderful, to tell you the truth, how are you feeling? Did you win?"

"I broke even, but I brought you something." Todd was grinning that grin that won me over every time, but also made me wonder what he was up to.

"What? What did you bring me? Leftover pizza? Not exactly what I had in mind for breakfast." I grinned right back at him.

"No, on the nightstand."

I rolled over and there it was, I stared at it for the longest time. "Aren't you going to say anything?" Todd asked.

"I've already peed today." I got out of bed. I wasn't exactly angry, it was more like I was terrified. We hadn't purchased a pregnancy test since the early days of trying to conceive and they had quickly become the enemy, never reporting back what I so badly wanted to see.

"Hey, I didn't mean to upset you. I just thought with the doctor's message we should find out. No sense waiting until Monday when we could celebrate all weekend."

"Or cry. I'm sorry Todd, but I just don't have it in me. I can't do it, but even more than that, I don't want to do it. I just want this weekend, not to think, not to worry, if something wonderful waits for us on the other side, we'll find out. Right now, I'm okay with not knowing."

I knew Todd wasn't okay not knowing, but I just couldn't bring myself to take that little plastic stick in the bathroom and pee on it. If, and that was a huge if, this was our turn, I wanted to know beyond a shadow of a doubt. I didn't want to spend all weekend wondering if that little ten dollar test knew what the hell it was talking about.

We stayed home and just relaxed. Bryan said Janie was doing okay, but she asked us to give her few days, she was trying to readjust to her life. Julie called but we decided to rent movies and just snuggle for most of the weekend.

On Monday, I called Dr. Garcia's office and asked for my test results.

"Hold on one second, Dr. Garcia just walked in." The nurse pushed the hold button and I was cut off from the conversation. What was going on? Shit, I had gotten my hopes up and now they were going to dash them. I braced myself for Dr. Garcia's news.

"Jeanie?" Dr. Garcia's voice came across the phone line.

"Hello Dr. Garcia, how are you?" What the hell? I was acting like we were having cocktails and chatting about the weather. Good manners die hard.

"I'm good, how are you? Where have you been? I heard you haven't called in until today."

"I explained that to the nurse but I'm calling in now. Someone left a message about an ultrasound?"

"Well, that's usually the next step, but we are getting ahead of ourselves. Jeanie, your blood work came back positive. Your HCG levels are just what we would expect for this stage of pregnancy."

I was stunned. I held the phone, my mouth hanging open, unable to speak. "Jeanie? Jeanie, are you still there?"

I swallowed hard and managed to say "Yes, yes I'm here. Pregnancy? Are you sure? Do you want me to come to in so you can run the test again? I would hate to waste the sonographer's time. I can be there…"

"Jeanie, the test is not wrong, this is not a line on a stick, this is blood work, levels of hormones in your body. When can you come in for your sonogram?"

I picked up my day planner and looked at my week. I had several meetings scheduled for the week and a training meeting all day Thursday. "Tomorrow looks like the best day for me, the easiest to rearrange." I still could not believe we were having this conversation.

"Let me give you back to Lisa and she will schedule it for you. Congratulations, this has been a long time coming." I hear the phone being handed off and Dr. Garcia telling Lisa, move what you have to, she can come in tomorrow.

"Hey Jeanie, congratulations! Is morning or afternoon better for you?"

“Umm, either, but morning if possible. I, I just, I can't believe this.”

Lisa laughed, “You wouldn't believe how many times a month I hear that! Okay, I can get you in at 7am, will that work?”

“Yes, I'll make it work. I'll be there, I mean we'll be there. Are you sure?” With a laugh Lisa said they would see me in the morning. I worked the rest of the day in a daze, I completely forgot to call Todd and let him know. Luckily, he called me so he was able to rearrange his schedule the following day. Todd was a little upset that I kept this to myself but I really was not able to process it at all so I did what I always do, push it away.

When I got home from work Todd was already there. I could hear the shower running. Where does this man get his energy? I feel like I still haven't recuperated from the week that Janie lost the baby. I kicked off my shoes and settled on the couch. I'll just take a quick nap before he gets out of the shower. I had barely closed my eyes when Todd was waking me up. He was standing next to the couch in a towel.

“Come on, get ready, we are going to celebrate!” Todd said, looking like a five year old who had been promised ice cream.

“Celebrate?” I just wanted a nap. “What are we celebrating?”

“Don't tell me you're not excited? Let's go have dinner in a nice restaurant, you know once the baby is born we won't just be able to go out to dinner any time we want. Things will change, we'll eat at places with play lands and toys in the meals.”

“You can't be serious.” I rolled over on the couch, away from him and his energy.

“I'm not going to take no for an answer. I made reservations at that French place we keep saying we want to try, so put on your little black dress and let's go!”

I got off the couch and got ready. When Todd gets like this nothing dissuades him. All he wanted to talk about at dinner was the baby. I was quickly growing tired of it.

“What if they are wrong? Can't we just wait and see? Doctors and tests are wrong all the time. I'm not sick, I don't feel any different. I really think they're wrong. Please don't get your hopes up”

That kind of put a damper on the night. I felt bad. I wanted to share his excitement, I really did, but something told me not to get my hopes up.

In the morning we had breakfast together, something we never do during the week, and headed to the hospital. We went through the check in process and just a little bit of joy was starting to stir. We've never done this before, never gotten this far. Could it be, after all this time, maybe, just maybe? I tried so hard not to think about it.

The nurse called us back, gave me a gown and told me to undress from the waist down. A technician I had never seen before came in and explained the vaginal ultrasound procedure. She turned the machine on, punched something into the key pad then put a condom on the ultrasound wand. I lost it, I started laughing. I had to sit up, I was laughing so hard I thought I might pee on the table.

“I'm sorry, it's just so.....funny. And I really have to pee now.” I hopped off the table with Todd and the technician both looking at me like I'd lost my mind. I went into the hall and found the restroom. It took me a few minutes to get myself under control so I could go back in the room.

“Okay, sorry, I just, I can't even explain it.”

“Happens all the time.” the technician said. She smiled, but Todd still looked like he thought I was crazy.

I got back up on the table and assumed the position. Todd reached for my hand and I closed my eyes. I didn't want to see what I knew wasn't there. Ultrasound techs are notoriously silent people. They rarely tell you what's going on, they look and then they let the doctor look, I knew that from going to appointments with my sisters.

I could hear her clicking stuff here and there but I still didn't open my eyes. After a few minutes she told us the doctor would be right in. I opened my eyes and looked at Todd. He shrugged his shoulders.

“I don't know how they know what anything is in there. It just looked like different shades of gray, I certainly didn't see a baby.”

“You wouldn't see a baby, if there is one there it's so tiny that the only thing we will see is a heartbeat. I'm not even sure how they are able to see that.”

Dr. Garcia walked in the room, put his gloves on, threw a new condom on the wand and patted my knee. “Are you ready?”

I just smiled, how do you answer that? I'm flat on my back, naked from the waist down with my legs in stirrups, what did he think I was doing? Again, I closed my eyes. When he told us he was wrong, I didn't want to see the disappointment on Todd's face.

Suddenly, there was a sound, and it grew louder and louder, until it filled the room. I opened my eyes and looked at Dr. Garcia, he was smiling.

“There you go, look at the screen, your first glimpse of your baby. Heart beat is strong, everything looks perfect.”

I looked at Todd and then at the screen. All I could see was a little white dot that was flashing. There's a baby in there?

“I don't see it?” Todd was leaning over me, trying to get closer to the screen.

“See that flashing little point? That's the baby’s' heartbeat, that is how it shows on an ultrasound. Strong, fast, and steady, just like we expected.”

I stared at the screen, praying, hoping, that this wasn't some cruel joke. That little blinking light was my baby? I didn't realize I was crying until Todd brushed away my tears.

“We did it, sweetie. We are going to have a baby.” He hugged me. Dr. Garcia turned off the machine. “Congratulations. Now, the next step is to go to your obstetrician.” He shook Todd's hand. “Hope to see you guys back here in a few years for number two. " He smiled and walked out of the room.

I clung to Todd. We had waited so long. I still couldn't believe it. Todd waited while I got dressed and as I was finishing up the technician came back into the room.

"Congratulations. Here are a few things for you, the first is baby's first picture, and because it's a little hard to see, here is baby's first video. It's a video of the baby's heart beating. Dr. G thought you would want it."

I clutched those two things to me the whole way home. Now, two months later, I was on my way to have lunch with my sister, those two things tucked safely in my purse. How am I going to tell her? Todd and I had decided not to tell anyone until I was twelve weeks pregnant and I insisted that Janie be told first. I had already told Julie but swore her to secrecy, not even Scott could know. I knew Todd couldn't wait to tell his family but I felt like I was going to tear Janie in two with this news.

I knew she would be happy for me. I knew it was going to hurt her, not just because of Lily. That would hurt enough, but because it was a reminder of what she couldn't have. Realistically I know that my sister is lucky to have four healthy kids, but I also know that my sisters' kids are lucky to have her for a mother and that she could have loved ten more, happily.

I pulled up in front of Jungle Jim's and looked for Janie's van. I found it and parked next to it. I knew she made an extra effort to be on time, not easy to do with four little ones, but she also knew I had to get back to work.

I walked into Jungle Jims and looked around for Janie, before I found her Lacey found me and came running. “Auntie Jeanie! Mommy said you were coming.” She took me by the hand and led me to the table, proud to have spotted me first. I hugged all the kids and they ran off to play again.

"I ordered the pizza, it should be here soon, and I got us salads too." Janie smiled at me. "Sister, you look like you lost your best friend, are you okay?"

I looked at Janie. I couldn't tell her, I just couldn't. She was finally starting to get some of that Janie spark back but you could see the sadness in her eyes still, I don't want to be the one to interfere with her healing.

"Tired, busy as hell at work, wondering how you are, other than that, I'm good. How are you doing?" The waitress arrived with the salads and I dug into mine.

"I'm good, really good. It's been so nice to talk with Ginny about Lily and her son, she knows exactly how this feels. I think it's helping."

"I'm glad you found someone to talk to. Julie and I try to understand but you're right, we really don't. How is Bryan doing? The kids seem to be fine."

"Bryan is so good, he has just jumped right in and not complained at all. There are still times when I just want to get in a bath and cry. We try to talk every night, about Lily, about how we feel, about what this means for our family. It's really been hard for me to accept that there will be no more babies."

When Janie said that I was sure I had made the right decision to not tell her, she wasn't ready to hear about my happiness yet. "I know sister, I know how you feel about babies, and you have such beautiful ones."

"What about you sister, what's going on with that?" In the nick of time the waitress brought the pizza and the kids came running over. Saved by a barrel of monkeys. Janie and I got to work dishing out pizza and drinks for everyone, Porter decided he wanted to sit in a chair like the big kids, no high chair for him today so we put him on the chair between us and finished our lunches.

I don't know how Janie does it, someone is always spilling and dropping and making a mess, it seemed like we were both in constant motion just wiping and picking up.

"Let me help you herd these cats back into the van," I looked at my watch, "I need to get going if I'm going to make my meeting."

We rounded up the kids, paid the bill and headed to the parking lot. Once the kids were safely buckled in I gave my sister a hug. "I love you Janie. Please, if you need anything, call me. You know I'm always there for you."

"I know sister," then she smiled that Janie smile, "So when are you gonna tell me?"

I felt the color drain out of my face. "Tell you what?"

"Come on sister, I've known since I came home from the hospital. I just want to hear you say it."

“I don't know what you are talking about. I gotta run, I'll call you later.”

“Jeanie, please, don't hide your joy from me, let me be part of it. It's okay sister. Sometimes bad things happen but that doesn't mean something good won't follow. Please?”

My eyes started burning with tears, “I’m really pregnant, Janie.” I reached into my purse and pulled out the picture and the DVD and handed them to her.

“Is this the baby?” she was holding up the DVD. I nodded. “Let’s put it in the kids DVD player so they can get their first look at their new cousin.”

Before I could stop her Janie was leaning into the back of the van and soon the sound of the baby’s heartbeat filled the air.

“What's that Mommy? That's not a Disney movie.” Collin said.

"No, baby boy, it's not. That is your Aunt Jeanie's baby. It's in her tummy, just a tiny little seed but that sound you hear, that's its heart beat."

Janie hugged me with tears in her eyes. "Sister, I'm so happy for you. And for me, I love being an aunt, but if you please, I would like a niece to spoil. I think we have it covered in the nephew department, time to even things out a little."

I hugged my sister. I had been so afraid to tell her, and she was happy for me!

"Now I know what to do with all of those boxes in the basement. There are lots of hand me downs coming your way sister."

I quickly hugged Janie and waved at the kids. "I gotta go, I love you." I turned and walked away, not trusting myself to say anything more. I cried the whole way back to work. What a hormonal, emotional mess I've become.

In the same hospital

Life has a way of moving on, even when we think the hurt is so great that there is no way to go on, we do. Every day gets a little easier, everyone said that but I didn't believe them. I couldn't imagine a time when it wouldn't hurt so bad it took my breath away. Today it is not as raw, the hurt is still there, an ache that I don't think will ever leave.

In the beginning I could hear her cry. I would wake up in the night and look for her, wanting to comfort her, to feel her warm little body against mine, to hold her. I know now it was my comfort I was looking for, and when I couldn't find Lily I would go to one of the other kids. I'm sure at times I was smothering them, but I couldn't help myself. I became afraid that I would lose the other kids so I refused to let them out of my sight.

So much to do every day, all the little mindless things that are part of being a wife and mother, and all the wonderful things, make the time pass. I found myself laughing again, at first it felt strange, and disloyal somehow, like if I was enjoying myself it was because Lily meant less to me. Every day she seemed to get farther and farther away. I struggled to remember her face, the feel of her skin. I would find myself studying the pictures of her.

Day after day marched by until one day as I was tucking in the kids I realized I hadn't thought of her at all. Then I felt guilty, what kind of mother doesn't think about her baby? It's a fine line you walk, mourning the child you lost and loving the ones you have. What is the right amount of grief that doesn't affect your children? How unfair is it to your children to be unhappy every day? And by doing all you can to keep your grief from affecting them are you shortchanging the child you are mourning?

I was amazed that time passed as quickly as it did. Every day I look at my babies and they are working to become the people they will be one day. Collin reads to his siblings now, really just parroting books he has memorized. Lacey is a second mom to Porter and Brie, Brie is fully potty trained and Porter, my last baby, is talking and making his wants known. He is quite the opinionated little guy!

Julie and I are driving to Jeanie's to help her labor. Jeanie has had a completely uneventful pregnancy, she felt good and looked so beautiful. Jeanie is using the midwife who delivered my babies at the same hospital. She wanted as much choice as possible but the security of all the bells and whistles at the hospital. Part of her birth plan is to labor at home as long as she can with her sisters by her side.

When we get to Jeanie's it feels so much like when my babies were born. The lights are low, candles are burning, soft music is playing and Jeanie is walking. Todd lets us in, he looks nervous.

"How is she?" Julie asks.

"She is doing well, doesn't seem to be in too much pain, still about seven minutes apart. I don't know what to do for her."

"Not much you can do." I said, "How are you?"

"Me? I'm fine."

Jeanie walked into the room, "There you guys are, geez, you took long enough, did you think I was going to be in labor all night?"

Julie and I looked at each other, "Yes" we said in unison and laughed.

"How are you sister?" I asked as I hugged her.

"Good, nervous, scared, nervous, crazy, I want it to hurry up but I want it to take forever. Does that make any sense at all?"

"Yes it does." Julie said, "I remember when I was in labor with the boys I wanted it to stop or at least slow down, while they were in my tummy I knew I could take care of them. Once they came out, all bets were off, I wasn't so sure about my abilities then."

I looked at Julie, “I felt the same way when I was in labor with Collin but I can't ever imagine you being unsure of yourself when it comes to your boys.”

We settled in for a long night. We made tea and walked and talked and tried to get Jeanie to nap. She wouldn't, but we did convince Todd it was okay for him to get some rest. He napped on the couch because he didn't want to be too far from Jeanie.

Jeanie wanted to hear our birth stories again. She was there when all of the kids were born so this stuff she knew first hand, but now she wanted the nitty gritty. How bad is it going to hurt? When should she get her epidural? Should she get the epidural? The questions just went on and on until finally, Jeanie was ready to go to the hospital.

We loaded up the cars with everything we thought Jeanie and Todd would need. The hospital was close, and Julie and I made small talk but all I was thinking about was the hospital. This was the same hospital where Lily was born and died. I have happy memories of this place from my other births but it is Lily's that's taking up space in my head right now. I just needed to hold it together for Jeanie.

"Janie? Are you even listening?" Julie asked.

"Sorry I was just thinking, what did you say?"

"Nothing important. Are you okay?" Julie looked at me. "Oh sister, I'm sorry, I didn't even think about how hard this might be for you. You don't have to do this you know, Jeanie will understand."

"No, it's ok. I was just thinking about Lily. It's going to be hard but it will be okay. I can't imagine not being there for Jeanie. It's just the hospital..."

"Well, we're here. Are you sure you are going to be okay?" Julie looked concerned.

“I'm fine, let's go meet our niece. I'm so excited to get a niece, I know you have two but this is my first.” I got out of the car and started walking toward the hospital.

Once inside, things moved at the pace of Jeanie's body. We did what needed to be done. We rubbed her back, we walked with her, fed her ice chips, and encouraged her when she felt she couldn’t go on. Todd watched all of this, never letting go of Jeanie's hand, trying to anticipate her needs.

The midwife was in and out, visiting with us, talking about what happens now, what Jeanie can expect, what Todd can expect and how he can help. Jeanie was a trooper, refusing any intervention. Julie reminded her to think hard about the pain meds because there would come a time when it would be too late and the choice would be taken from her.

I walked the halls in the hospital, wandered past the nursery and looked at all the sweet little babies. When it got too much I called Bryan and checked on my babies, even Porter said love you on the phone.

Finally, Ava was ready to be born. Jeanie assumed the position of millions of women before her and started the hard work of helping her baby into the world. Todd took his place at Jeanie's knees and Julie and I each took a side by her head. Todd, under the midwife's guidance, was going to catch his daughter as she came into the world.

Jeanie pushed and pushed, following directions like a pro. I was fading in and out. Each sound, smell and sight brought back my births. I wasn't really conscious for Lily's birth and in my mind everything was becoming jumbled. I was sad that I missed that. The very first sight of my child was lost to me, and would be forever.

"I can see her head, honey!" Todd said excitedly, "Keep pushing, she is almost here."

Julie and I were holding Jeanie up with pillows and trying to encourage her without it becoming too much. I remember very well being into the hard work of pushing a baby out and having someone touch me too much or talk too loudly. When you're working that hard everything is intensified.

Suddenly, there she was, my sister's first child. Todd caught her and held her up for Jeanie to see, the three of us were hugging and crying. The midwife helped Todd lay the baby on Jeanie's stomach while they cut the cord, and then Todd walked to the head of the bed to join his family. I couldn't see through my tears and when I looked over Julie was crying just as hard. Jeanie had waited so long and been through so much to get here. Seeing her with her daughter was the most beautiful sight in the world.

A nurse took the baby to clean her up, get her vitals and wrap her in a blanket. Todd went and stood watch over her, as if he couldn't bear to be away from that little girl.

"She's so beautiful, and perfect, and amazing and strong, and..." I was crying too hard to come up with any more words.

"Oh, sister, are you okay, is this too hard for you? I know you must miss Lily even more today." Jeanie, always taking care of me.

"These tears aren't for Lily. I thought they would be. These are for Ava, I always cry when our babies come because I'm always amazed that God, the universe, whatever, thinks we are worthy of these children."

The nurse handed Ava to Todd and he carefully walked over and handed her to Jeanie. Seeing my sister with her baby for the first time was a beautiful thing. Julie and I cooed over her, took a million pictures and cried some more.

"Let's go get some coffee and give these guys their first taste of time alone with that little girl" Julie said.

We went to the cafeteria talking about Ava and our babies.

"At times like these I want another baby so badly." Julie said with a sad smile.

“Then you should have one. The boys are older now, I understood when they were little why you decided not to have another one, twins are a lot of work, but now, they could even help you.”

“No, it's not practical. Scott and I decided when we got married that we only wanted two kids, although I do think he would love a daughter, but going back to diapers and sleepless nights, no thank you!”

“You loved it and you know it. Think about it, talk to Scott. If you really want it then you should, otherwise you might always regret it.” I said, grabbing my coffee and a muffin. I was starving.

We sat at a table and ate our muffins then got a refill for our coffee so we could go back upstairs. On the way up we detoured to the nursery and looked at all the beautiful little lives in there, just getting started, so full of promise. I hoped they all had sisters, what would I do without mine?

We knocked lightly on the door and walked in. The midwife was talking with Jeanie, trying to help her get Ava to latch on and Ava was rooting for all she was worth and letting out these little tiny mewing cries when she couldn't find what she was looking for. Todd was standing there beaming at his wife and daughter, I took a few quick pictures. That's my gift to the kids, I can't sing or tell stories but I can capture their stories in picture, and I do, every day.

After Ava latched on and nursed for a minute or two, she drifted right off to sleep. Being born is hard work.

Jeanie motioned us closer to the bed, “I think it's time she met her aunts.” She looked at me and I leaned down to take Ava from her arms.

I looked at my sleeping niece and then at my sister. “You do good work sister, she is beautiful. Thanks for giving me a niece, she is perfect.”

I kissed Ava's forehead, “Hey there sweet baby girl, where have you been? We have waited such a long, long time for you, and as your Momma would say, you were definitely worth the wait little Miss Ava.” I looked at Jeanie and Todd, “Her name fits her perfectly, she looks like an Ava.”

Reluctantly I handed her to Julie so she could get to know her. I got out my camera and started taking pictures. It's easier to distance yourself through the lens of the camera. The look on Julie's face when she looked at Ava, so filled with longing. The love shining from Jeanie and Todd for each other and this little life they had created. The tiny, soft little fist of my niece curled around my sister’s finger. So many moments make up a memory, so many memories make up a life.

I missed Lily so much, I really missed all of my babies because they weren't with me, but I missed Lily the most. When you lose someone, you lose all those moments and this was a reminder of moments lost. Lily and Ava would not play together and nap together and pull each other's hair. They would not share secrets and sleepovers.

Looking at my sisters through the camera I was reminded how grateful I am that they are in my life. How truly blessed we are as a family, and it just keeps getting better.

Dreams do come true

When I woke up it took me a minute to remember where I was. I looked over and saw Todd sleeping in the chair next to me, the hospital bassinet with my daughter in it between us. She's really here. My baby, my daughter, finally. I watched them both sleep, still amazed that this had finally happened to me. I had really given up on carrying and delivering my own child, I didn't think that was something that was going to happen in this lifetime. There had been too many disappointments, and yet, there she is, sleeping soundly, swaddled in a hospital blanket.

I thought back over the last twenty four hours. I was someone's mom. Now I could participate in all those things my sisters did with their children as something more than an aunt. I am a mom. It still seems surreal.

As if she knew I was staring at her, Ava started to wiggle. I reached for her but before I picked her up she made that little mewing noise that my sisters have warned me will soon turn into a very loud cry. Todd heard her and sat straight up, concern on his face.

“Is she okay?”

“She's just waking up, want to hand her to me?” I said. I watched my big husband pick up our tiny daughter, the sight brought tears to my eyes.

“What's wrong? Do you hurt?” he said, handing Ava to me.

“No, nothing is wrong, I’m still just amazed that she is here. Our daughter. A baby that grew in my body. Now I understand why Janie kept having babies, I want ten more!” I laid Ava on the bed and checked her diaper, it seemed impossibly tiny.

“Can you hand me a diaper and the wipes? I think she needs a clean bottom before she eats.” It seemed to take forever to change her,

I was so afraid that I was going to hurt her. She held her little legs close to her body and I had to pull on them to get the old diaper off and the new one on. Ava continued making those little mewing sounds, not at all a happy camper.

The diaper was changed and I got to work figuring out how to get her to latch on. Neither one of us was very good at this. Ava cried and rooted around, my nipple seemed way too big for her tiny mouth. When the nurse came in I was in tears as well, I could not get my daughter to latch on and she was really crying now.

“It's always hard at first, don't believe what anyone tells you. Sometimes the first couple weeks are incredibly hard, but you guys will figure it out.” She came over and changed my positioning of Ava a little and stuffed my nipple in her mouth. “Sometimes you just gotta stuff it in there. Once it's in, she knows what to do.”

She was right, Ava started nursing like a pro, her little fists balled up next to her cheeks and staring straight at me. The nurse checked all my vitals and asked about wet diapers, when was the last time Ava ate, and if I needed anything.

“Enjoy today, get as much rest as you can, because tomorrow we will boot you out of here.” she said with a smile. “If you are tired, let us take her to the nursery. This is the only time you get to nap while professionals watch over her, take advantage of it.”

I said I would, but knew I wouldn't. I was never going to let Ava out of my sight. I could see by Todd's face that he felt the same way.

After Ava had her fill and drifted off, Todd and I just watched her sleep, quietly talking about tomorrow, when we could go home with our daughter. I couldn't wait and was afraid it would seem to take forever to get here. While we were talking our pediatrician came in. Dr. Pennington was Janie's pediatrician too and I loved the way she was with the kids.

“How is our girl?” She asked looking at the baby.

"She's wonderful, just got a full tummy and fell back to sleep." I said.

"Well hand her over, mom, this is the best part of my job, getting to know them when they are brand new." She took Ava from me and stared into her little face. "She's going to be a beauty."

I'm sure she says that about all the new babies but I still felt so proud, like she passed inspection. Dr. Pennington put her in the bassinet and unwrapped the blanket that was around her.

"Her Apgar's were very good, her weight is excellent, sounds like labor and delivery weren't too hard on her." She was checking her umbilical cord, taking off her diaper, moving her this way and that. Ava woke up and started fussing. "Everything looks wonderful, no tub baths until this falls off," she said pointing the umbilical cord. "Did the nurse tell you how to take care of that?"

"Yes she did, does it hurt her if I move it?" That stump of an umbilical cord looked sore and scary to me.

“No, it doesn't hurt her, don't worry about that. And it may start to smell a little funny, don't worry about that either. She put Ava's diaper back on. “She's perfect, good work Mom and Dad. Call my office and make an appointment for two weeks. We want to make sure she is gaining weight like she should be. Bring all of your questions and if anything comes up before then that you don't want to wait for, just call and talk to my nurse. She can answer most things and if she can't, I'll call you back. How is the nursing going?”

“It's hard, I'm afraid we are not very good at it.” I said.

“Most first time moms aren’t, and you have to remember, this is all new for her. Up until now she didn't have to work for what she needed, it was all provided for her. If you have any problems or questions about nursing you can call my nurse also, we encourage you to breast feed as long as possible, it's good for both of you.”

Once Dr. Pennington got Ava's diaper back on and swaddled her again, she quieted right down. “Alright, have fun with her and I'll see you in two weeks.” Dr. Pennington said as she was leaving.

I looked at Todd, “Another first, a doctor came into this room and talked to us about our child. Everything about this is so amazing to me. I keep thinking, this is the first time I've done this as a mom, this is the first time this has happened since Ava was born, I wonder when that wears off?”

“Maybe when the second one is born.” Todd said with a smile. He started talking about what we needed to do to get Ava home tomorrow and I found myself drifting off again.

The rest of the day passed pretty quickly. Ava and I tried to find a rhythm with this nursing thing, it really was hard. I would get so frustrated that I was reduced to tears and the nurse would come in and help. Thank God for those nurses, otherwise poor Ava would never have eaten.

In the morning I couldn't wait to get out of there. I felt like we were waiting to start our life as a family. Todd had gone home, picked up the car seat, installed it and had one of the nurses make sure he did it right.

When he got back I had everything packed and ready to go. The nurse brought a wheelchair, Todd grabbed my suitcase and Ava's diaper bag and we were headed home.

Pulling in the driveway I started to laugh. My sisters had been here. There was a stork stuck in the front lawn with Ava's information on it. The house looked like it had been wrapped in pink crepe paper and there was a huge banner over the front door that said "Welcome home Mom, Dad, and Ava"

We went in through the garage and the inside of the house was just as decorated, with flowers, pink crepe paper, and balloons. Thehe whole gang was there waiting for me. I hugged my sisters, and then all of my nieces and nephews. It was so good to see them all, to have them share in this but I really just wanted to be alone with my husband and daughter, in our home, for the first time.

We let each of the kids sit on the couch and hold the baby. That little girl got so many kisses. I tried not to worry that the kids were passing on germs but part of me was made a little crazy by all of those kids holding and kissing her. Maybe it was just because I was tired.

Julie must have known how I was feeling because before too long she started wrapping things up.

“Okay, let's get ready to go. Aunt Jeanie worked really hard to get Ava here and now she needs to rest. Kiss your Aunt and Uncle and let's go to Aunt Janie's and have lunch.”

Another round of kisses, mostly for Todd and I this time, although one or two still fell on Ava's little head. I thanked my sisters and headed for the couch.

“Oh, dinner is in the fridge, spaghetti, and there is garlic bread too. Also the freezer has dinner for a week, the list is on the front of the fridge. Not that you are getting rid of us for a week, but we just wanted you to know not to worry about fixing anything, everything just has to be heated up. Call if you need anything.” Julie said on her way out the door. Of course Julie would have made sure that we were taken care of and could just relax with Ava.

By the time my sisters and the kids left I was tired again. Todd settled me on the couch and Ava into the cradle and almost before he was done I was asleep again.

As the dust settles

"Hey, want to stop and get p-i-z-z-a for the kids? I don't feel like making anything." I said to Julie as we were buckling the kids in the car.

"Does Aunt Janie think I don't know how to spell pizza?" Sam asked his mom, always the serious one.

Julie laughed, "I think Aunt Janie was just practicing her spelling." she looked at me, "Guess those days are behind us now, huh?"

"Certainly sounds that way. I'll call ahead and order pizza and just have them deliver it, no sense unbuckling everyone to pick it up. See you at the house." I got in the van and backed out of the driveway.

Something was wrong with Julie, I'd been trying to figure it out ever since we were at the hospital when Ava was born. I guess she will tell me when she's ready. There is no pushing Julie, she always has a plan and will not tell you until she is ready.

I called and ordered pizza, one cheese and one meat lovers. Our boys were definitely carnivores. I listened to the kids talking in the backseat and wondered what was going on with Julie. She was different lately, more relaxed, but tenser at the same time. Julie was the sister that organized everything, she had always taken care of us. There were times when I resented it when I was younger. I didn't need my sister telling me what to do. My mother couldn't be bothered, so why should Julie? As I got older I came to appreciate all the things Julie did, often at the expense of herself, like the food for Jeanie. After being up all night with Jeanie, Julie had still gone home and cooked like a madwoman so Jeanie wouldn't have to worry about it once she got home.

Julie pulled in behind me and we set the troops loose. We sent them into the backyard to play until lunch. I wanted to ask Julie what was going on but I knew it would be pointless.

In the house I started a pot of coffee and mixed up some lemonade for the kids. Julie and I took Porter into the yard so he could run with the rest of the kids. He was at that age where being the youngest was making him mad. He wanted to run with the big kids, be allowed in the yard by himself, which would happen soon enough. For now, I was cherishing his babyness.

Julie and I talked about our new niece and how happy Jeanie looked. It was about time she had a baby, that girl had wanted one for years and each disappointment took some of the joy out of her. We had been afraid she would never get that back. Ava, all seven pounds of her, had given Jeanie back her joy.

The doorbell rang and I went to get the pizza while Julie got the kids inside. Lunch was crazy, as it always is with six kids. Julie and I spend most of lunch time laughing at them. Our boys always had the craziest ideas. Max was the daredevil, Collin the brains, and Sam, well, poor Sam, he was the worrier. Collin would come up with a plan, Max would be raring to go, and Sam would think of all the things that could go wrong. Usually Sam was right, Max or Collin would get a bump or a bruise and wear them like battle wounds, and Sam would be sad that no one listened to him. Today, they were talking about building a fort out of boxes, then Max decided it should be a tree house. To Sam, that had disaster written all over it.

Finally lunch was done and we herded the kids to naps. We knew the older boys would just sit in Collin's room and plot. Porter and the girls would be asleep almost instantly, so we had about two hours of uninterrupted sister time.

In the kitchen I poured us each a cup of coffee and sat at the table with Julie. I started to ask her about our sister day the following weekend when she interrupted me.

"I'm leaving Scott." Julie said.

"What?!" I almost choked on my coffee. Julie and Scott had always seemed perfect for each other, they were both organized and efficient, they left nothing to chance.

"I know it will be hard for everyone to understand but you guys don't really know Scott, you only know the Scott he allows you to see." Julie sipped her coffee as calmly as if we were talking about the kids outgrowing clothes.

"Sister, I... I didn't know. If there was a problem, why didn't you tell us? Maybe Bryan or Todd could have talked to Scott, gotten this all straightened out."

Julie started telling me what her life was like with Scott. I couldn't believe it, my sister, who always made the right decisions and took care of everyone and everything, was being treated like a child in her marriage. No, not like a child, parents didn't talk to their children the way Scott talked to her. I listened and couldn't help but think how true it is that you don't know anyone's marriage if you haven't lived in it. I always thought Julie and Scott were happy. They seemed happy, the boys seem happy, they have a good life. How wrong I was.

When Julie finished I was crying. She wasn't. I guess she was so used to this life that it didn't have the ability to hurt her anymore.

“I always thought I would stay. I didn't want the boys to come from a broken home, I thought I could make it work, but I was wrong. Scott has always been so good with the boys but lately I can see it, I can see him turning his perfectionism on them. I think since I stood up to him and refused to move to Nebraska he has been trying to get at me through the boys. Poor Sam, you know how timid he is, and how Max always takes the lead. Scott has been calling Max a bully and telling him that he isn’t going to have any friends, and then he tells Sam that no one wants to be friends with a sissy. My poor boys are so confused. It's only happened a few times but I can see it’s affecting them already. When Scott is home, Max tries so hard to keep all of his ideas to himself because Scott will pick them apart, tell him why it will never work and how stupid it is. Sam just tries to stay out of his way.”

“Oh, sister, I'm so sorry. I can't imagine having to listen to him belittle the boys.”

“Yes, it's hard and the first time it happened I waited until the boys went to bed, I never question Scott in front of anyone, not even the children. When the boys went to bed I asked if he had a bad day, told him I thought he was a little hard on them. Boy was that the wrong thing to do. He lectured me for hours about what a bad mother I was and how our boys were going to be useless when they grew up because they had me as a mother. The next day he was even harder on them. Since then I haven't said anything, just try to limit his interaction with them."

"Why don't we have the boys sleep over the next time Scott is home? You know they can come here whenever you want them to." I couldn't think of a single thing to say to my sister, I was still stunned by all that she had told me.

"That would be perfect, sister. The next time Scott is home I'm going to tell him I want a divorce. It will be better if the boys aren't there. Something snapped inside me when Jeanie had Ava. I've always been a little jealous of how you are able to be the mother you want to be, and I know that Todd will allow Jeanie to be the mother she wants to be. My boys and I deserve that too. Sam and Max already ask me why they can eat what they want at your house but never get to choose at home."

"I'll be with you when you tell Scott, Bryan will keep the kids." I told her.

"Thanks sister, but I have to do this on my own. Besides, I don't want to involve everyone. This could get ugly and regardless Scott is still the boys' father and will be a part of our lives so I don't want there to be any hard feelings or uncomfortableness."

"What can I do? I don't even know how to begin to help you." I asked her. "I can't believe how calm you are about this." I said "If it were me, just thinking about leaving Bryan and being on my own with the kids, I would be terrified."

"I've been planning this for a long time. If I'm honest, it's been in the back of my mind since before the boys were born. I tried not to get pregnant, I took my birth control for a year after Scott thought I stopped, I did not want to have kids, and, I'm embarrassed to admit this, but... when the boys were born part of me resented them, I thought they would tie me to him forever and I would never get away. I never realized that my boys would suffer too, and I let it happen." Julie looked down at her coffee cup.

"Julie, your boys haven't suffered, they have a wonderful life. They don't know what you've been through, you've shielded them from that." I was still stunned.

"They don't know what Scott is like, but they have suffered. I know it's all little stuff, like not being able to choose what they want for lunch, or when they want to read or play with the Legos or run in the yard. You and Jeanie tease me about running a military academy and the sad thing is, it's true. That's what it's like for my boys. If they don't wake up at 7:00, I wake them up, if they aren't hungry at 6, too bad, eat now or be hungry. Everything they do is according to his schedule, what he believes is best for them to turn them into responsible, productive citizens and good fathers and husbands. If I let them watch an extra half hour of TV and he finds out, the next day they get no TV, or Lego time or whatever it is that I did that wasn't according to schedule. I have to put a stop to it. I think they are still young enough that I can show them it's okay to have fun."

“The boys will be fine, kids are resilient, but what about you? Are you going to be okay? Are you sure you can support the three of you?” I asked.

“Yes, I actually have quite a bit of money in savings. Scott would never let me spend the money I made writing and now between my blog and writing for that column I make enough that I don’t need to touch that money.”

“Have you told Jeanie and Todd?” I was still stunned.

“No, I wanted to tell you and Bryan first, Jeanie and Todd need to get settled with that new baby girl. But I plan to tell them before Scott comes home again. He’s only been gone a week so I have a while until the next surprise visit.”

“Julie, I don't know what to say. I'm sorry you have gone through this alone for so long. I should have been able to see that you weren't happy.”

"I did a good job of hiding it. Initially I thought it was because we were young and trying to figure things out, I thought once he saw that I was competent and didn't need constant direction he would back off. Things have just gotten worse. The sad thing is ,I think I would have continued to put up with it if he would have left the boys alone. He's always been a good father and they adore him."

I heard Porter calling me from upstairs, I looked at the clock, I couldn't believe we had been talking for over two hours. "Sister, anything you need, anything at all, you know we will all be there for you." I went to get Porter and tell the boys they could come downstairs.

How does this happen? Not only that, how does it go on for ten years without anyone noticing? How lonely Julie must have been. I was determined to be a better sister. Together, Jeanie and I would help Julie and the boys get through this. All we've ever really had was each other, and it was always Julie taking care of us. Now we would get the chance to take care of her.

A Note from the Author

Thank you! I hope you enjoyed reading this as much as I enjoyed writing it. If you would like to know about upcoming book releases and occasional free books at well please sign up for my newsletter by clicking here.

You can also visit my website, www.carolpaxman.com, or find me on Twitter or Facebook.

If you would like to leave a review, head to Amazon or Goodreads and help other people find this book.

Made in the USA
Middletown, DE
28 August 2019